## "You think the killer is targeting painters of sunrises, don't you?"

Brigitte fastened her seat belt.

"I think it's possible. Other than gray eyes, nothing else fits. We have women in their twenties, thirties and forties as victims. We can't be sure how or where he targeted them, but Los Artes is known as a hub for artists. Either way, artistry might be a good place to help us narrow down the hunting ground."

He turned the ignition, but the engine didn't roll over. Nothing but a click.

"Alternator? Battery?" Brigitte asked and fanned her face.

"No," Duke said, his stomach forming a knot. It didn't sound like either. The click was different. Like something had been locked into place. "Brigitte, get out of the car! Now!"

At the same time, they opened their doors, and as Duke's foot hit the pavement, a deafening boom and a wave of intense heat seared his back as his feet lifted off the ground.

Did Brigitte make it out of the car?

**Jessica R. Patch** lives in the Mid-South, where she pens inspirational contemporary romance and romantic suspense novels. When she's not hunched over her laptop or going on adventurous trips with willing friends in the name of research, you can find her watching way too much Netflix with her family and collecting recipes for amazing dishes she'll probably never cook. To learn more about Jessica, please visit her at jessicarpatch.com.

### Books by Jessica R. Patch

### Love Inspired Suspense

#### *Quantico Profilers*

*Texas Cold Case Threat*
*Cold Case Killer Profile*

#### *Cold Case Investigators*

*Cold Case Takedown*
*Cold Case Double Cross*
*Yuletide Cold Case Cover-Up*

#### *The Security Specialists*

*Deep Waters*
*Secret Service Setup*
*Dangerous Obsession*

### Love Inspired Trade

*Her Darkest Secret*

Visit the Author Profile page at LoveInspired.com for more titles.

# COLD CASE KILLER PROFILE

## JESSICA R. PATCH

**LOVE INSPIRED** SUSPENSE
INSPIRATIONAL ROMANCE

# LOVE INSPIRED® SUSPENSE

## INSPIRATIONAL ROMANCE

Recycling programs for this product may not exist in your area.

ISBN-13: 978-1-335-55510-6

Cold Case Killer Profile

Copyright © 2022 by Jessica R. Patch

For questions and comments about the quality of this book, please contact us at CustomerService@Harlequin.com.

Love Inspired
22 Adelaide St. West, 41st Floor
Toronto, Ontario M5H 4E3, Canada
www.LoveInspired.com

**Printed in U.S.A.**

And she called the name of the Lord that spake unto her,
Thou God seest me: for she said, Have I also here
looked after him that seeth me?
—*Genesis* 16:13

To my agent, Rachel Kent. You saw the writer in me and have been such a source of encouragement, hope and friendship. When I see you, I see Jesus. Thank you.

Special thanks:

To my awesome editor, Shana Asaro.
You keep making my books better.

To Susan Tuttle, who, as always, brainstorms like a boss and tells me when I'm off the mark and always makes time for me. Your friendship is golden.

To Jodie Bailey for always being there to give me great distractions, pep talks and reasons to laugh when I really want to cry.

To the retired rock star Desoto County CID detective (among a whole litany of titles you've achieved in your career) Jerry Owensby for helping make my call-ins authentic. Anything I missed is on me.

# ONE

Any other woman might recoil at the chilling howl of the cunning and opportunist coyote, but not Brigitte Linsey. She welcomed the enhancement to the artistic atmosphere as she painted during the predawn hours.

Visiting the Chihuahuan desert before sunrise, alone, could be considered foolish, but Brigitte grew up nearby in Los Artes, West Texas, and she knew this terrain well. Respected the creatures that inhabited the landscape, and relished the scenery from the Sierra Madre—gorgeous mountains flanking the desert—to the pools and oases teeming with life. She'd captured it all, even the mountain lions, kit fox and mule deer.

But her favorite rendering was the landscape at sunrise—new each morning and never the same. When life was challenging—pretty much every single day—and her job as a patrol officer with the Los Artes PD presented her with the world's most inhumane acts, she could rely on coming out in the quiet while the temperatures rose from freezing, but before it became blistering, and painting the waking desert. Painting the pinks, purples, oranges and yellows on the horizon.

She had created dozens of desert paintings, especially since her mom passed two years ago and Dad's Alzheimer's had taken a fast downward spiral. She needed the beauty because so much was ugly. Disease. Despair. Grief. Painting returned some life and joy.

Brigitte tucked a paintbrush between her teeth and tied her painter's smock around her waist. She'd already set up the easel and put the fresh canvas on. Once the sun fully peaked, she'd lose all she wanted to capture and the August heat would force her to trek back to the road she'd parked on and leave until the next opportunity.

Growing up, Dad had encouraged her art and put her into specialized classes in middle school. Presently, Brigitte had a few hangings in local galleries downtown and had sold about twelve pieces, but her job as a city officer and forensic artist for the county didn't offer her the necessary time to make a career out of it. So she did both—made the world better through hobby art and catching bad guys, though in Los Artes crime wasn't quite as heavy as larger cities like El Paso or even Lubbock.

Another howl unleashed and she surveyed the area, keeping her gun in her apron just in case. Twilight was on the move, bringing a purplish hue to the desert and revealing pops of light in contrast to the pitch-black night—except for the few glorious stars overhead, which were slowly disappearing, like Dad's mind. When the diagnosis was given, Brigitte had decided to stay on at the family home. She'd moved back in after her mom's cancer diagnosis, hoping they could reconnect. Their relationship had never been bad, it just hadn't been good.

*Distant.* That's the only way she knew to describe

Mary Linsey. She'd kept everyone, including Dad, at arm's length.

But that year hadn't repaired or brought them any closer. Brigitte had felt as alone as always when it came to Mom.

And now with Dad...she truly was.

Last evening, he kept calling her Mary, her mother's name, and apologizing.

The last apology Brigitte heard was from Will, an officer she'd been involved with from Gran Valle, a neighboring town. He'd apologized that things hadn't worked out between them, especially since he'd felt like it had been going somewhere more permanent.

But Brigitte didn't do permanent. Permanent didn't always make for happy.

Dad was proof of that.

He'd always told her she'd find the one for her like he found Mom. But what Brigitte remembered was Dad loving her mother and her mother not equally returning that love.

No, thank you. Brigitte didn't want to enter a marriage where she loved more. She felt alone enough already.

Even Dad barely knew who she was these days, and it crushed her—the early onset. He was too young for this fatal disease.

The wind blew her hair in her face, and she pulled it back with a hair tie she wore as a bracelet. A shade of purple and yellow in a sea of desert brown and olive green caught her eye about a hundred feet west. Completely out of place. She frowned and studied it. What was that? A dress? She moved toward the object before her brain caught up and warned her something was off and dangerous. Chills ripped up her spine and she shivered as she closed in on the material fluttering in the morning breeze.

Stunned at first, Brigitte gasped, and then her police training kicked in and she inched forward with caution, careful not to contaminate the crime scene. And it was a crime scene. Before her, a woman a little younger than Brigitte had been laid out as if relaxing. Long blond hair and wide, slate-gray eyes stared up into nothing. Her hands rested casually on her lap, and her legs stretched out in front of her as if she was here to watch the sun rise.

The sunrise.

Brigitte's stomach roiled. This was the same MO as the Sunrise Serial Killer. It had been years since he'd murdered—six, maybe? She'd hoped he was dead or in prison due to the long stretch of silence. He was known for strangling and posing women in desert surroundings. But that wasn't the only thing odd with this young woman. On the ground beside her lay a gold brooch with an emerald-cut ruby in the middle. A blurred memory flashed in her mind.

*Are you painting, Daddy?* Red hands.

*Yes. Yes. Go to your room.*

She blinked out of the thoughts and confusion, pulled her cell phone from her painting smock, and called 911, but the reception was shoddy out here. She gave Dispatch her location, ended the call and further inspected the brooch. Why had it tugged a random and fuzzy memory from her? Was that a real memory? Dad had never been an artist or painter. Why would he have been painting without her? Without gloves on, she refrained from touching and contaminating the scene. No purse. No wallet.

Rustling snapped her to attention, and a man who felt solid as granite rushed her, knocking her to the desert floor. He wore a dark jacket, pants and ski mask, but his eyes were darker than night. His lips curled back in a snarl. His gloved hands wrapped around her neck, and she dived into her apron pocket for her Glock, but it had fallen out in the tumble to the ground. She worked her thumbs into his eyes and pressed. His grip released, and she sucked in precious air and kneed him in the groin, wiggling her way out from under him.

Scrambling to her feet, she pitched forward and bolted toward the road where she'd parked her Jeep. Behind her, footsteps increased in speed, and she pushed into a sprint, shoulders hunched as adrenaline raced through her veins, awakening her flight mode.

So close to freedom.

Sirens wailed, and she pressed on without glancing back. Couldn't allow herself to slow down now. The sound of being chased halted, but still she kept going.

"Brigitte!"

Her name being called by the good guys gave her a measure of relief as she reached her Jeep and the police.

Gratitude washed over her, and she hugged the first officer on the scene, a cop from Gran Valle. Tony Jackson—a friend of her ex-boyfriend, Will. He hugged her tightly, but briefly. Other first responders headed for the desert to comb for the killer. The forensic team approached in their Tyvek suits and kits.

She pointed the way, then gave her statement to Tony.

"You really shouldn't be out here alone, Brigitte. That doesn't seem smart."

Spare her the lecture. She'd been doing this for the past five years. Never once encountered anything more than a wild animal. Close call with a Mexican wolf once. But that's it. She didn't reply to his warning and followed him to the body. Already, markers had been laid out and the vic's hands put in paper sacks to preserve potential evidence. Yellow crime-scene tape cordoned off the area. She slipped under it and accepted a pair of gloves from a tech.

"Huh. That's odd." She studied the victim then knelt.

"What's that?"

"There was a brooch lying beside her, and now it's gone." The scene had been preserved and she was fairly certain it hadn't been kicked out of the way during the fight, but she slowly and carefully walked the perimeter in case.

"I don't see a brooch, Brigitte." Tony pointed to the victim. "I see a ring on her right middle finger. That's all. You sure?"

She wouldn't have been had she not had that weird memory flash. "I'm sure." How bizarre.

"Are you saying he stopped chasing you, doubled back and pinched the jewelry? Seems risky with sirens signaling our arrival."

Brigitte squeezed the bridge of her nose. "I don't know." But that was the only explanation. The killer had slowed enough and risked being caught for that one piece of jewelry. Why? Had the victim been wearing it and he wanted it as a trophy? Many serial killers kept sick mementos from their victims.

Now that the sun had risen, she spotted tire tracks. Small, like a Gator or ATV. "Look. He must have parked like I did on a back road and driven the body into the desert."

"What do we got here?" a deep voice bellowed, and Brigitte turned. A large man in a hoodie and sweats approached.

"Hey, Detective Collins," Tony said through a chuckle.

Detective Collins glanced down at his attire. "I run in the desert every morning. Heard the call on my radio. When I heard 'Sunrise Serial Killer,' I beelined it for my car and headed over." He held out his beefy hand and squinted into the sun, the lines around his eyes crinkling and giving away his late middle age. "I'm the lead homicide detective with Gran Valle. This'll be my case, since this part of the desert is in Gran Valle jurisdiction. You find the body?"

"I did. Officer Brigitte Linsey." She shook his hand, then gave him the same briefing she'd given Tony.

"You said you saw a piece of jewelry?"

"Beside her."

"Interesting. We'll need a formal statement. Glad it was a trained officer out here and not simply an artist. Good work staying alive." He nodded once and made his way over to the CSI techs.

"Come by in an hour or so to the station in case we need more information."

*Ugh.* Hopefully she wouldn't run into Will. Awkward. "Sure." He walked her to her Jeep, where she buckled up and drove onto the road. Media was already swarming and salivating over a new Sunrise Serial Killer story. She was glad to have bolted before they peppered her with questions.

Once she reached Los Artes, her lungs released and she exhaled as the reality of how quickly she'd almost been ended hit her. No one would be there for Dad if she died. A sudden need to see her father enveloped her, and she rushed to the assisted living center.

Chill bumps dotted her arms and the hairs on her neck prickled like a cactus as she clambered from her vehicle. She scanned the sparse lot but couldn't shake the feeling that unseen eyes roamed over her every move.

Maybe coming here hadn't been wise.

Would the killer want to finish what he started?

Warning bells rang and echoed against her brain. She was more than a witness to a crime scene. She was the woman who'd gotten away. Would a serial killer allow that?

Fear raked her throat with acid as the bloodcurdling thought stabbed against her skull.

No. No he would not.

She might have become his new prey.


FBI special agent Duke Jericho unfolded himself from the rental car and stared at the L-shaped building with potted ferns flanking the automatic sliding doors of the assisted living center. After landing in El Paso from Quantico and driving to Gran Valle for a quick briefing and command post setup, he decided to talk to the witness who'd been attacked early this morning personally. An Officer Will Talbort had shared she might be at the Sunny Days assisted living center visiting her dad. For an officer in a neighboring town, the man seemed to know a lot of personal information about Officer Linsey, and it didn't take a great profiler or Sherlock Holmes to make the deduction they were or had been romantically involved.

He stood under the breezeway, a reprieve from the dry Texas heat, but Duke didn't mind hot weather. He was originally from Mobile, Alabama, so he was accustomed to sweltering temps and high humidity. He'd ditched his tie on the plane and left his white dress shirt unbuttoned at the collar. He shrugged out of his suit coat and laid it over his arm. He wasn't one to intrude on a personal situation, and visiting her father—who was diagnosed with early-onset Alzheimer's, according to Officer Talbort—was pretty personal, but Duke had a job to do, and it wasn't like he hadn't tried to reach her by phone for a heads-up. No answer.

Kenny Riley, the behavioral analyst who'd originally worked up the Sunrise Serial Killer profile, had retired two weeks ago, and all his assessments and paperwork had landed on Duke's desk. And with his other former colleague—and one of the best in the biz—Chelsey now living in El Paso and working as a consultant for the Texas Rangers, he and his remaining colleague, Vera Gilmore, had taken the lion's share of the extra work.

But Chelsey had finally found her lifetime partner and had gotten hitched a couple of months ago to a Texas Ranger—a good egg. And Duke couldn't fault her for that.

He was here with fresh eyes and to make any necessary tweaks to Kenny's profile, which had been done well over a decade ago. It had been six years since the SSK last struck. Why such random time frames between kills?

He popped a spearmint breath mint, crunching right in with a loud pop, then he tucked a second one against his cheek to melt. When he entered the establishment, the smells of lemon and a hint of mothballs hit his senses. It was a more upscale living and rehab center than he'd been in before, with large, fresh bouquets of flowers on the tables in the lobby. Residents visited and chatted. The women working behind the moon-shaped desk grinned and welcomed him. He showed them his creds and asked to be directed to Brigitte Linsey.

The woman with bouncy red curls tapped on the computer. "She's in the east wing. Room 308."

Her gaze held, and he smirked as her pupils dilated. Duke wasn't vain, but he wasn't stupid, either, and he'd never had trouble attracting women. Unfortunately, he was a terrible judge of character—irony right there, when he made his living judging character and reading people. When the person of interest was a criminal, one could easily be objective. But matters of the heart were a whole different animal, and he had divorce papers to prove he was no good at marriage—or, more aptly, marriage was no good to him.

He moseyed toward the east wing, reading the signs pointing the way. His pastor told him to give himself more grace. He supposed he ought to. After all, he wasn't the one who had an affair and ran off with not only his best friend but the best man from their wedding. It wasn't him who had lied for over a year, then refused to get counseling and go back to church and their faith that they'd let fall by the wayside. Duke had done everything he knew to do, and it hadn't been enough.

But he had received counseling and *he* had gone back to his faith. Four years strong now. Sometimes he felt the dull ache of failure. Feelings of self-doubt and guilt. Why hadn't he been able to fix it? Why hadn't he seen the signs? What could he have done differently?

Room 302…303… A soft, soothing female voice

stopped him in his tracks. The kind of voice that read children's bedtime stories.

"I feel so helpless and powerless. He's fading before my very eyes, Mrs. Kipling. One minute he's talking to me with clarity, and the next he's asking where Mary is. It's so hard to say she died. I'm all alone." A sniff. Blowing of the nose. He really shouldn't be eavesdropping, but he couldn't help himself. The voice soothed him, and her words sent a blip into his chest. He felt them clear into his marrow. Felt the helplessness. Powerlessness.

*Alone.*

"Honey, I'm so sorry. He was a wonderful father. Take those memories. Cherish them. Write them down. Remember."

"I wish I had someone to lean on."

"Oh, doll, you can lean on me. I may not have my sight, but I have two shoulders. Bony, but able." A raspy voice laughed. "And you know you can lean on God."

"I know. But sometimes it's hard to feel His invisible shoulders."

He bypassed the room and knocked on room 308. "Mary, is that you?" a man asked. Duke stepped into the small studio room. The TV played *M\*A\*S\*H*. Duke expected to see an older man, but this guy looked to be in his early fifties at best.

No sign of Officer Linsey. "Mr. Linsey? Is your daughter here?"

"Maybe. Are your intentions honorable?" he said with a fatherly gruff and grit that Duke admired.

"Yes, sir, they are. I only would like to have some company and conversation with her. Won't even keep her past supper." The word sent a rumble into his stomach. It had been hours since he'd eaten anything, and supper time was fast approaching.

The man's dark eyes lit up, and he laughed. "Good answer, my boy. Good answer."

*My boy.* No way was Mr. Linsey old enough to be his father. "Is she around? Maybe in the restroom or getting some coffee?"

"Who are you?" he asked, confused.

"My apologies. I'm Duke Jericho. I'm here to see Brigitte." Her name rolling off his tongue sounded strange and oddly intriguing. "Is she here?"

"Who? I don't know no Brigitte. Who are you?"

"What's going on?" The same voice that had lured him moments ago now spoke, and Duke turned. A petite woman in bright colors with long, dark hair falling in waves down her shoulders in a total '70s look glared at him.

He held up his credentials. "Special Agent Duke Jericho. I'm here about what happened earlier today."

"Mary. What happened today? Are you okay? You're not hurt, are you?" Mr. Linsey stood.

"No, Daddy. I'm not Mary. I'm Brigitte. I'm not hurt. Sit on down. Be comfortable." The man obeyed but scowled.

"Where's Mary?"

Officer Linsey sighed. "She's not here right now, Daddy."

"When will she be back?"

"You can see her soon. Watch your show. It's *M\*A\*S\*H.*"

"I like that show. Alan Alda is a fine actor. Funny, too." He pointed at the TV, and Brigitte adjusted the afghan across his lap and frowned.

"Has no idea who I am, but knows a Hollywood actor. Nice." She whirled around and shot Duke another menacing glare. "In the hall, right now."

"Yes, ma'am."

"Are you mocking me?" She squinted, hands on her hips.

"No." He laughed and held up his hands. "You just brought out the schoolboy in me with that tone."

"He's here to ask for your hand in marriage. His intentions are honorable." Mr. Linsey nodded once, and Brigitte's cheeks tinged a lovely shade of pink.

"Yeah, well, I'll be the judge of his intentions," she bit off and eyed Duke again, then stalked into the hall, her flowery perfume wafting in the air and dizzying him. What was that? Jasmine? Honeysuckle?

Boy, she was mad. Duke had an imposing presence and had often used it to his advantage with criminals, but Brigitte Linsey had no fear. No sense of intimidation, but clearly a temper hotter than Texas in August. Fascinating. Amusing. He'd barely stepped into the hall when she poked a finger straight into his chest.

"Who do you think you are, coming in here and disrupting my father? He is a sick man. You've confused and upset him. Do you have any idea how long it took me to calm him down when I got here? He was disoriented and combative. You could have called my cell phone."

He had, but he decided against revealing that when a finger was in his chest and the woman was on a roll.

"We could have met at the precinct or even a coffee shop."

"You want to have me coffee with me?" He couldn't help himself. It was inappropriate and agitating and she'd been through the wringer, but he couldn't control his tongue.

"I want to have *words* with you," she said, not missing a beat or batting an eye. Quick off the cuff. He liked her spunk.

"At a coffee shop?"

Her nostrils flared, and her eyes narrowed. He may have pushed it too far. "What do you want?"

"I'm here to tweak or work up a new profile on the Sunrise Serial Killer. I have a command post set up in Gran Valle. And I did call your cell phone."

She reached for her back pocket, patted her backside with both hands, then closed her eyes.

"Guess you didn't have your phone on your person."

She huffed and rubbed her temples. "They have a game room down the hall. We can talk in there."

"Do they have coffee?" he asked and smirked.

Her lips worked into a flat line. "Decaf. If you count that as coffee."

"I don't."

"Then they have water."

"I like water."

She pointed toward the fork in the hall. "On the right. I'll get them."

He entered a large, rectangular room. Round and square tables dotted the big open space. Two men played a game of chess, and a flock of women were playing cards. The table for two by the window was empty and secluded. He chose that one and sat facing the door.

Brigitte entered with two bottles of water and the same scowl she'd left him with. For almost dying today, she was in full form. Maybe it had miffed her more than terrified her. Guess he'd find out. He studied her gait, her facial expression.

She was resolute. Focused. Irritated, but the slight tremble in her right hand gave away the fear she was working hard to mask. He'd back off riling her up—or what might be borderline flirting. It was unprofessional and inappropriate. Brigitte handed him the water and sat across from him but shifted her chair slightly to see the door. Occupational hazard—never knew who was coming in and what they'd be bringing. He twisted off the blue cap and pulled a long swig.

"Would you mind telling me what happened today? And before you say, 'read the report,' I have. I want to hear it from you."

She sipped her water, then walked him through this morning's events. The brooch angle was interesting. It had been risky for the killer to pause and nab it—he agreed.

"Why do you think he took it?" His question was more to gauge her as a law enforcer. He had his own ideas.

"I suspect he needed it as a trophy. It's not uncommon for serial killers to take one. It's possible he dropped it when he heard or saw me coming. But he couldn't resist leaving it. Even with the risk."

That's what Duke thought as well. "I agree."

An awkward silence hung.

"You go back to the precinct for further questioning?"

She shook her head. "The detective on the case didn't call me. I've been here most of the afternoon. Didn't want to…" She shrugged.

"Be alone."

She glanced at the door. "There's a woman here I've befriended. Her son comes on the weekends, but she needs someone, too. She's blind—glaucoma. That's why I wasn't in the room when you arrived. I've been chatting with her."

Being comforted, but she didn't want to share that or speak to his suggestion of being alone. Instead she prattled—nervous or a gesture when she was embarrassed. Interesting.

But he got it—the need for motherly comfort. He'd let his mother treat him like a little boy when Deena had walked out. Crumpled right on her shoulder and cried. She'd run her hands through his hair and told him it would be okay. That God would heal him and turn the mess into something good. He'd done most of the healing. Hadn't seen the good quite yet.

"I should tell you something else," she said, drawing him out of his painful thoughts.

"What's that?"

"I think I was followed here earlier. And…and maybe that's why I haven't had the nerve to leave just yet. I know I need to. I have to sleep some before my shift." She shrugged as if it was nothing, but for the first time, he saw raw terror in her eyes, and to avoid frightening her more, he didn't tell her that she probably had been and that the killer had a score to settle now. She'd rushed him. Interrupted him. He wasn't going to let her get away with that.

"Well, then I'll follow you and make sure you get home safely."

She pinched the bridge of her nose. "I'm a cop. I shouldn't be afraid. And I can take of myself."

He nodded, believing every word. "You survived

today. That tells me you're fast on your feet and re-sourceful. Trained and skilled. But I disagree about the fact you shouldn't be afraid. Fear can be healthy and keep us safe. It kept you inside and not out there alone. So…let me escort you home. Help you clear the house. Then I'll go."

She studied him, as if weighing his words as truth or lie. She nodded once. "All right."

As they walked out the sliding doors into the heat, a cold slithered through his bones.

Officer Linsey had good instincts.

Duke himself could feel them being watched.

# TWO

Sunrise became sunset sooner than Brigitte would have liked. Something about the stretch of darkness tonight unsettled her—usually she preferred the night shift, and it was convenient for now.

After Agent Jericho had helped clear the house, he lingered, asking further questions about the attack. She recognized excuses when she heard them. He'd been concerned for her safety, and rightly so. However, she was trained and a pretty good shot. Finally, she'd let him know that if she was going to work later, she needed some sleep.

It was nearing midnight now. Only a few more hours until her shift ended at 7:00 a.m. Her zone covered the downtown district, which was fairly quiet. Her partner would be nearby, patrolling in his car. Terry Inland was a good guy. Wife and a little one on the way. Total family man. She envied what he had—but not enough to allow her heart to be vulnerable and rejected or abandoned. Brigitte had quietly witnessed her own father's sadness when he didn't think anyone was watching. If all his efforts to keep the love alive hadn't worked, then how could Brigitte have a fighting chance? Besides, civilians didn't always love her job, and cops she'd dated didn't get her artistic side. Still, she continued to date— she wanted the companionship, until it got too close to her heart, and then she tanked it. Every. Single. Time. What a hot mess.

Her radio crackled, and Myra the dispatcher's voice came through. "Unit 20?"

"Unit 20."

"We have a 10-62 and a possible 10-64 at 2120 Main Street. Stu's Garage. A man called, says he heard clanging inside and a woman's scream."

That was in her zone, and she wasn't far. A breaking and entering and possible woman in distress in a mechanic's garage this late? That wasn't going to be good. "Unit 20. Any weapons or anything else in the area I need to be aware of?"

"Unknown at this time, Unit 20."

"Ten-four."

Adrenaline kicked in as she made a U-turn on the dead two-lane highway leading through Los Artes and rushed to the scene, slowing as she reached the mechanic's shop. No light inside, not even a flashlight beam. JJ's Hardware and a greasy spoon flanked the gunmetal-gray building with grimy picture windows. Parking on the curb, she exited the vehicle as Terry approached.

"And I thought it was going to be a quiet night," he said.

"Maybe it's teenagers and a girl screamed at a rat or something." Too much death and horror already. Let it be pranks or a party of kids getting too wild.

She pulled her Maglite and weapon, and they approached the side street joining the diner and the garage. Terry motioned to follow him around back, and she nodded. Brigitte held her gun steady, but her ticker hammered against her ribs like it'd pop out of her chest any minute.

A bird fluttered and flew off the gutter. The back door was open.

Terry exchanged a glance with Brigitte, and she nodded again that she had his back. He entered the building, gun poised, and she moved along behind him, scanning the dark garage, the smells of oil and something coppery coating her senses. Tools and car parts littered the filthy concrete floor, and she maneuvered around the maze, hoping not to alert anyone to their presence.

The atmosphere changed. Darkness hovered and hairs on her neck rose. "I don't like this," she murmured.

"I don't, either. Something feels…wrong."

Scuffling drew their attention to the far east corner. "Los Artes Police. Hands up—"

The flash of a gun firing lit up the dark like a firecracker, and the garage echoed at the deafening pop.

Terry returned fire as he collapsed on the grimy floor. Brigitte ducked for cover while scooting toward her partner. He was too quiet. Too still. Her hands trembled as she scanned the dark garage and checked for a pulse.

She hit her radio and called it in. "Unit 20. Officer down at 2120 Main Street. Stu's Garage. I repeat, officer down and in critical con—"

Another bullet unleashed, and Brigitte cried out as the searing burn ripped up her shoulder. Blindly, she fired, hoping to keep them safe and contained. He'd hit her in the left arm, thankfully, and she still had her gun in her right.

Tools clinked and clanked on the concrete, and she fired toward the noise, only seeing a shadow race along the far wall. "Help is coming, Terry. Hold on." He didn't speak. Blood pooled and mixed with oil on the floor, and in the minimal moonlight streaming through the windows she saw blood oozing through his uniform. He'd taken a chest shot. Unable to give chase, she put pressure on the wound. "Stay with me, buddy. Hold on." Sirens wailed. "Hear that? That's the cavalry. Just stick with me. Think of Patricia and your little one coming into the world."

Terry's hand covered hers and squeezed, then lost its strength.

"No, no, no! Don't you close your eyes. Stay with me!" Lights, voices and equipment invaded the garage, then the paramedics worked on Terry and put him on a stretcher. Another set of paramedics checked out her wound. Nothing but a burning graze to the left shoulder that required some antiseptic and a bandage. Her captain, Donnie Boyett, was in a T-shirt and jeans, a deep crease from his pillow running along his right cheek.

"What happened, Linsey?" he asked in his gruff tone, but it was threaded with concern.

She briefed him while the police searched the garage and Stu, the owner, came racing inside, but her colleagues forced him out. This was now a crime scene.

"Did you find a woman?" she called out to a fellow officer. "Dispatch said the call was about hearing a woman in distress. Thought someone was hurting her. But we only saw one figure. A man, by his build."

"No woman, Linsey. Sorry."

She tucked a hair that had fallen from her ponytail behind her ear and scanned the garage, avoiding the pool of her partner's blood. She stomped outside and bent at the knees. Captain Boyett followed her, laying a hand on her shoulder. "I just talked to Dispatch. Call was anonymous. Burner phone. We can ping a cell tower, but that isn't going to help us other than reveal a wide reach."

Acid burned in her gut, and she inhaled deeply for fear she might throw up. "You think this was a setup by the Sunrise Serial Killer, don't you? To lure me in and take me out." But he'd gotten Terry in the cross fire. Collateral damage. If Terry died, it would be all Brigitte's fault.

"I do," he said gently. "And before you go blaming yourself—"

"Too late."

He sighed. "You had no idea. This isn't the way he normally plays."

"We don't *know* how he plays, because he's never been interrupted before that we know of. I should have been thinking ahead." Or taken the lead into the building.

"No, I think I will come through." A gritty, deep voice carried through the crowd, and Brigitte looked up as Agent Jericho showed his creds to the officer and ducked under the crime-scene tape. He wore a pair of worn jeans, frayed at the edges, and a white T-shirt that hugged a muscular torso and slender waist. His thick, dark hair showed signs of sleep or a man distressed, and his five o'clock shadow with pops of silver increased his menacing appearance.

He spotted her and time stilled for just a second as her breath caught. He cautiously approached, a fierce, protective eye roaming her. "Are you hurt?"

She cleared her throat. "No."

He gave her another quick glance, and his eyes grew dark. "No?" He pointed to her shoulder.

"Well, I mean in comparison."

His jaw worked and his nostrils flared.

Captain Boyett introduced himself. Agent Jericho briefed him on why he was on the scene, and Cap brought him up to speed, but Brigitte barely listened. Terry was in the hospital. Fighting for his life. She needed to be there. Needed to be with Patricia, but how would she face her?

"I'm going to the hospital. Has anyone called Patricia?" Gran Valle General was the closest hospital to them, and she wasn't standing here another minute.

"Curtis is on his way to inform her, give her a ride to Gran Valle General. I imagine most every officer from the day shift is there. I need to stay here for now, but I'll be by later. Take the rest of the night off. We'll get someone to cover you."

Brigitte didn't protest. Her mind was going in a million directions and she'd be no good on patrol.

"I'll follow you," Agent Jericho said.

"No need, Agent—"

"Duke. Call me Duke."

She held his dark gaze and nodded. "Duke, then." His set jaw and squared shoulders said all she needed to hear—the man wasn't backing down or planning to listen to her objections on following her to the hospital.

Slipping under the yellow plastic tape, she headed to her marked unit and turned her light bar on, racing to Gran Valle, Duke right behind her in his rented Altima. She parked near the emergency department, leaving her lights flashing, and Duke pulled up behind her, clambering out of the vehicle—too small to comfortably hold his presence. He grimaced and shook his knee, and she imagined a track or more likely football injury. Not built like a linebacker but a quarterback.

Brigitte entered, gained the necessary information she needed and headed to the OR waiting area, but Duke held her back.

"What?"

He pointed to her hands, arms and uniform. "You want his wife seeing that?"

She hadn't thought. "No. No. Let me clean up some." She hurried to the restrooms and washed the blood off her arms, hands and face, then did the best she could with what had transferred to her uniform. At least it was a dark blue, so the blood wasn't quite as shocking.

When she exited, Duke nodded once, and they entered the OR waiting area. Patricia hadn't arrived yet. Several friends and colleagues were gathered, conversing about what they wanted to do with the creep that shot down a brother in blue.

Brigitte answered their questions and they rallied around her, all commending her for doing her job, but that didn't calm her nerves or ease her guilt. She didn't feel part of the gathering. She felt as always—alone.

They hadn't been there. They didn't have to feel or carry the guilt.

Duke stood in the corner, leaning on the wall with one ankle crossed over the other. Nonchalant and comfortable, but she noticed his sharp eyes surveying and his ear cocked, listening. She strode toward him, and his gaze slowly swung to her and her stomach dipped.

"I see you're an artist, too." She raised an eyebrow and bobbed her head toward the Los Artes cops.

"Yeah? How so?" Arms folded over his chest, revealing guns on both, he waited on her reply.

"You have paying attention while not appearing to pay attention down to an art form."

"Hmm." He held her stare one beat, two.

She shifted from one foot to the other. "Patricia—Terry's wife—is pregnant." She wasn't sure why she blurted it.

"You did everything by the book, Officer Lins—"

"Brigitte. If I'm calling you Duke, then…" She shrugged.

"Brigitte." He said it like molasses pouring out of a jar, as if testing it on his tongue. "Okay. You did everything by the book. I understand the feelings of guilt, missteps, fault and blame. I'd feel the same way, and probably most everyone in this room would, too, which is why they keep touching you, telling you that you did good. Because you did."

His words carried authority and years of experience. "You ever have a partner end up in critical condition and felt responsible?"

Shifting, he uncrossed his arms from over his chest and shoved his hands into the back pockets of his jeans. "In a way."

In a way? "What's that mean?" Dark hair drew her attention, and Patricia entered the waiting room with two of Terry's best cop friends. She wore loungewear and her hair was pulled into a messy bun, her belly about to pop. She spotted Brigitte, and Brigitte's mouth turned dry and a lump rose in her throat.

Patricia rushed to Brigitte and wrapped her in an embrace. "Oh, Brig. Oh, Brig," she cried and sobbed on her shoulder. "I'm so glad you were there. So glad you're safe."

She'd taken a graze, but she'd keep that to herself. "I'm so sorry, Patricia. I feel responsible. I have no words."

"Terry and I both know the risks of this job. Please don't apologize. You stayed with him." She noticed her bloodstains and her face paled, but she recovered quickly.

The doors opened.

A doctor entered. "Mrs. Inland?"

Patricia clutched Brigitte's hand. "Yes?" Her voice was weak and carried a tremor.

"I'd like to speak with you."

Duke sipped his third cup of terrible cop coffee and stared at the board he'd created only hours earlier. After leaving the hospital last night and escorting Brigitte back home, he'd had a hard time drifting to sleep in a hotel bed, knowing that a killer was after her, but she was capable and he had to trust her instincts. He really had no business feeling this protective over a woman he barely knew.

Terry Inland had made it through surgery and would recover, but there had been damage to his dominant arm, which meant he likely wouldn't be able to remain on the force. He could possibly work a desk. Brigitte hadn't taken that news well, but his wife had been relieved and thrilled he was going to live. Had to take the bad with the good.

Duke had gone to bed thinking about the bad. Brigitte had asked him if he had ever felt responsible for a partner's critical condition, and while he'd never experienced what many law agents did, he had experienced his ex-wife's critical condition. At that time he'd been a field agent and then trained and worked in the BAU. He was gone often. Buried in his work. He couldn't blame his failed marriage solely on Deena.

The door to the conference room opened, and the scent of flowers hit him first, then Brigitte entered wearing a pair of jeans and a V-neck T-shirt with swirls of colors on the front. It was nearing lunchtime. Dark circles revealed she hadn't slept much. Her hair was pulled back in a loose ponytail, and she wore little to no makeup. Fresh-faced and looking younger than her late twenties—he'd done some research on her. Told himself it was purely professional, but his curiosity was much deeper, more personal than that.

Turmoil brewed in her storm cloud–gray eyes.

"I didn't expect to see you." Though he was pleasantly surprised to do so. "News?"

"Not good." Brigitte heaved a sigh and plopped into a conference room chair, the air whooshing from the cushion. She glanced up at the board. "Wow. You've been busy."

"I'm here to work."

"Do you sleep?"

"Not much. You?"

"Not lately." She rested her hands on the faux mahogany table. "I've actually come to offer you my services."

Curiosity piqued. "Yeah? What services would those be?"

"Well… Cap put me on a leave of absence—with pay, of course. He's convinced the shooter in the garage is the Sunrise Serial Killer. The fact the call was anonymous and untraceable and was for my work zone—it makes sense. He's afraid he might try to lure me out again and next time something worse may happen. I'm a safety risk."

She frowned. "I get it. I agree. But, Duke, I can't sit around on my hands and not do anything. A killer is after me, regardless if it was the shooter in the garage or not. I have the chance to help stop him before he goes cold again, because I'm a target. He hasn't gone radio silent just yet like before. If he does, then we lose possibly years before he strikes again. I want him now, and since you're working alone..."

Duke understood her need to be useful. To keep busy. And he tended to agree with her captain. This killer had no real pattern to his timing. A year. Two. This latest was six years. Was he in prison? Were there cases in other states? He'd already run it through ViCAP. If there were any similar crimes, the Violent Crime Apprehension Program database would give them the info.

Unfortunately, he didn't want to work with Brigitte Linsey. She was a total distraction from her lovely face to her heady perfume. He worked with women often—daily, even—but they didn't affect him like Brigitte. He mentally kicked himself for being attracted to a woman so young. She was twenty-eight. Barely. He'd be forty next month.

But he was being a jerk. Not allowing her to work on a case because he was attracted to her was not only selfish but unprofessional. Not to mention if she was with him, he could keep tabs and keep her safe. She needed backup. "All right." He shoved a stack of photos toward her. "Those are victims' belongings. I've sent most of the evidence off to the lab in Quantico for retesting, including the DNA found on the jewelry—which could be his. We might get a match this time. We also uploaded some DNA to an ancestry site. We've found some good leads on cold cases this way through phenotyping. It's worth a shot."

"What do you think so far? Personally," she asked.

"He's meticulous and calculated and hates interruptions or monkey wrenches thrown in his plans. He may even have a mild form of OCD. Definitely thrives on routine and repetition. Otherwise he wouldn't have been so enraged that you infringed on his time with the victim, nor would he have risked swiping that piece of jewelry, knowing the police were closing in on him. He couldn't help himself. Which means if we keep throwing him off, he'll make a mistake."

Brigitte flipped through the photos. "Good. I hope he does." She pointed to the murder board he'd put together with victims and pertinent information. "I've lived in Los Artes my whole life, so I'm aware of his kills here and in the Gran Valle area, but only the more recent victims."

"Four victims that we know of, not counting Kayla Lowe, our most recent victim." They'd identified her about an hour after bringing her to the morgue. "All had gray eyes. It's the only common denominator I've found so far. First victim was discovered nearly eighteen years ago. Tina Wheeler." He stood and walked to the board, pointing to Kayla's picture. "I want to start with her, though. I'm treading lightly. Detective Chris Collins from Gran Valle is working lead on the case and has been the detective on all of the homicides but one. I don't want him to think I suspect him of doing a shoddy job, but I want to do my own investigation." The killer chose the Gran Valle jurisdiction to dump his victims for a reason. Best he find out for himself. Except Jamie Harker, the third victim, who was placed in the Los Artes jurisdiction, but close to Gran Valle.

Had the killer made a mistake by a few feet or had there been a reason?

A man poked his head in the door, dark eyes resting on Duke. "Am I interrupting?" Chris Collins held up a few files. Duke had done his research on him. He always wanted to know who he was working with. Built like the marine he once was, with broad shoulders and an intimidating stance, Collins was a force. Closed many cases. Most seniority on the force. Nearing retirement and lived in Gran Valle his entire life when he wasn't on a tour.

"Ears burning? I was just talking about you to Officer Linsey."

Detective Collins nodded once to Brigitte. "Officer. Good to see you again. You look like you have more color than last time we met."

"Well, no one is attempting to murder me at the moment."

He smirked then redirected his sight onto Duke. "Thought I'd bring in my personal notes on the previous victims." He handed them over. "You need anything, you let me know."

"Will do."

Collins lingered, then tapped the door frame twice and exited. Brigitte eyed the personal notes. "Are there any mentions of jewelry missing from the victims?"

He opened Detective Collins's notes, searching for anything about missing jewelry, but nothing had been jotted down. Guess he didn't connect dots or find it relevant at the time, personally. But Duke thought the idea of the killer taking jewelry held merit and was worth pursuing.

"No, but the formal reports noted Jamie Harker's

boyfriend asked about a pair of pearl earrings he'd purchased for her that she wore faithfully. The report and photos show her wearing small gold hoops that day." He raked his hand over his face, feeling every bit exhausted. "I don't know what that means except the boyfriend wanted to know where they were, which means they weren't on her. I called the family to ask about them. They never recovered those pearl earrings."

"So what happened to them?"

"I don't know."

Brigitte laid her big, square bag on the table and removed a manila folder. "I drew him. What I remember. Not much with a ski mask, but his lips are full and his eyes dark. Could be dark blue or brown. Sparse lashes. I don't remember them being long. Maybe it'll help somehow."

He took the paper and noticed the shading, the depth and realism of her drawing. "It's good. Really good. It'll help. Everything helps."

"Good." She cleared her throat. "Thanks for letting me work on the case with you, but you also have to know that my dad sometimes has episodes, and if it's during the day, I drop everything for him. At times, I'm the only one who can calm him down if he's combative. It's the main reason I stay on the night shift. So… I may have to leave sometimes."

"I understand. Family should come first. Always." He'd learned that the hard way. Suffered the consequences. Wouldn't make that mistake again or expect others to neglect the people they loved.

"You have family?" she asked.

"My parents live in Mobile, and I have a younger sister—married with two kiddos. Lives in Huntsville."

She bit her lower lip and rubbed her hand along her thigh. "You, uh…married?"

*Ah.* "No. I'm actually divorced. Four years. You?" He knew she wasn't, but he didn't want to clue her in on his cyberinvestigating. She might take it as stalking.

"I'm sorry to hear that. Marriages are hard. Not that I know from personal experience. Just what I've seen. So to answer your question, no."

Marriage was hard. And while it was supposed to be a guarantee for a lifetime, it wasn't. And Duke wasn't sure he wanted to go down the marriage road again. One more reason not to pursue romantic entanglements with women who wanted to be married. It would hurt them. "I'm sure you'll find the right man. Maybe that Talbort fellow."

Her eyes widened. "Why would you say him?"

*Busted.* "He told me where I could find you and why. I picked up on a personal connection."

"Once. But that's over. I don't really stay in relationships very long."

He wanted to ask why but refrained, wanted to keep the conversation going against his better judgment. "Would you want to grab lunch and go over some more notes?"

She hesitated. "I was gonna run some errands…"

Why had he asked that? Stupid.

"But there's a good deli near my house. If you don't mind stopping by there first."

"No problem." He grabbed his suit coat, then followed her to her house. She froze halfway up the walkway. Instinctively he pulled his weapon and met her near the porch. "What's wrong?"

"My door is cracked open."

Someone might be inside.

# THREE

Drawing her Glock, Brigitte glanced back at Duke, who was in position and ready for anything. Dread filled her gut. This was the exact setup from last night, when Terry had been wounded.

"Don't worry about me. Do your job," Duke said, as if reading her thoughts. "Focus."

She nodded and entered the small foyer, sticking to the walls and surveying. Nothing out of place at first glance. She moved to the kitchen on the right. The fridge hummed, and ice dropped into the holder. Duke stayed with her as she cleared the small laundry room, then the living room, master bedroom and the bathroom downstairs.

They then made their way up her childhood home's stairs, the wooden joists creaking. At the top were two more bedrooms, her dad's old office and another bathroom. Her breath hitched at a noise, but it was only the house settling.

After inspecting the rooms, her lungs opened and she inhaled deeply and hurried downstairs to examine the front door. No sign of forced entry. Nothing touched.

"Does anyone have a key?"

Brigitte stood dumbfounded. "Only Ray across the street. But he wouldn't have come in here for no reason, and if he had, he would have locked it back up." This was strange. She called Ray, but he didn't answer. Voice mail. She left him a message to call her. "Maybe I left it open this morning. I had a boatload of stuff in my arms, and I'll be honest, my mind wasn't exactly firing on all cylinders."

"Well, nothing is missing, and it's clear. How about I run to the deli. I assume it's the one we passed."

She nodded. "I should have offered to make something quick for us, but I'm not much of a grocery shopper." It shouldn't be a big deal, but heat filled her cheeks. "I kinda live off cheese and crackers or cereal, and I'm out of cheese and milk."

Duke chuckled. "No worries. The deli looked good to me."

"It is. I eat their club several times a week."

"When you're out of cheese and milk?" His crooked grin slid right into her chest and sent a flutter to her heart.

"Or when I'm not." She turned toward the kitchen. "I have coffee—something I never seem to run dry on. I can make a pot. I make a good brew."

"Perfect. How 'bout lock the door when I leave?" He winked and stepped onto the porch. Brigitte closed it and dramatically locked it for effect.

"Nicely done, Officer." Humor laced his raspy voice, and she snickered. How could she even grin at such a crazy time? Duke Jericho.

Hurrying to the kitchen, she laid her keys on the counter, keeping her gun just in case, and went to work brewing a full pot of French roast. She ordered the beans online and had them on a weekly shipment schedule. Maybe she should do that for milk and cheese, too.

The coffeepot gurgled, and the smell of rich coffee filled the kitchen.

Too much had happened since yesterday morning, and she was running on fumes, admittedly afraid. When she was little, her dad always chased away the bad guys in her imagination or her dreams. Now, he barely knew her name. And some days he didn't know her at all.

She was not only alone but lonely and wished for that closeness they'd once shared. It reminded her of happier days. Days she'd love to revisit. And she could. Duke would be gone for a few more minutes, which would be enough time to grab an album of her and her dad.

He'd loved photography as a hobby, and there were scads of organized memories. She headed upstairs and pulled down the attic door with a slow screech and unfolded the ladder. A wave of heat smacked her in the face.

Maybe she'd bring down a whole box instead of combing through them up here, where she'd likely have a heatstroke. Brigitte switched on the attic light on the wall, then climbed the ladder into the dimly lit room. Exposed insulation, evidence of rodents, old furniture and dozens of stacked boxes covered with dust filled the A-framed area. Some of the boxes had been knocked over, and contents spilled out.

Finally, she found several boxes labeled *Dad and Brig photos*. Duke would be back any time, which meant she needed to hurry up and get some boxes downstairs. He'd be locked out. Sweat rolled down her spine and dotted her upper lip and forehead.

She wiped her brow with the back of her hand, and

the stairs creaked. Snapping to attention, she listened while unholstering her weapon and carefully inching toward the attic ladder, leaving the boxes. Maybe she was being paranoid. The house popped and creaked often; she never paid it attention.

But a killer had never come for her until now.

She placed one foot on the ladder, pausing to listen, and then she descended it like stairs going forward, not with her back facing out and leaving her vulnerable. At the bottom of the ladder, she waited, watched. No one was on the stairs. Or in the hall.

Sighing, she holstered her weapon, heard the coffee-pot beep and turned to go back and bring down a box. She was on the fourth rung when she caught a blur in her peripheral vision. As she turned, a looming figure shoved her from the ladder, and she landed on the hard-wood with a thud, her head banging the wall. How had they missed an intruder?

He wore the same ski mask and was dressed in all dark clothes again. Menacing eyes latched on to hers, and his lips peeled back in a snarl. His gloved hands clamped around her throat, and he'd positioned his knees where she couldn't get to her weapon.

Duke would be here soon. Any minute.

But the door was locked, and the attacker was cutting off her air supply. She couldn't scream, but she thrashed and fought, working to pull off his mask to reveal his face. He jerked back and grabbed both her hands with one of his, pinning them over her head, then he wrapped his free hand around her throat and squeezed.

With her extremities pinned, she had no way to fight. Teeth. She had her teeth. She chomped down on the leather gloves, biting through them. He growled and released his hand from her throat. She stole the fleeting opportunity and rose up, headbutting him with all her might. The pain rang clear to her ears, but adrenaline drove her.

He reared back, and she scrambled up as a car door slammed.

*Duke!*

She ran for the stairs, leaping down them and to the front door, her fingers fumbling as she worked to turn the dead bolt. Flinging open the door, she raced straight into him. He dropped the plastic bag he held and touched her face, instinctively knowing trouble had come for her, and darted inside.

"Upstairs!" she hollered, but he was already taking them four at time. She came up behind him, her pulse spiking to dangerous levels.

Duke ran into the room directly behind the attic ladder and Brigitte followed.

The window was open, and he peered outside. "He went down the lattice into the backyard."

They rushed downstairs. "Let's comb the neighborhood. He couldn't have gotten far."

Brigitte leaped into the passenger side of Duke's rental, and they sped down the road, circling the block and looking for a man on foot or a car that might appear out of place, but it was a bust.

Duke reached over and grasped her hand. "Tell me what happened."

She went through the details as he circled the next block over just for something to do, to be useful. That's what she would have done. He drove down her street, and she saw Ray was carrying a rake, sweat dotting his brow as he approached the front yard. "That's my neighbor. Slow down."

Duke rolled his window down, and Brigitte leaned over. "Hey, Ray."

"Hey, Brig." His dark hair was disheveled, and he looked out of breath. "What's going on?" He eyed Duke.

"I tried to call you."

"Oh. Sorry. I just got in. Been hiking all day in Big Bend. 'Bout to do some gardening." He cocked his head. "You okay?"

"You haven't by any chance seen anything or anyone strange around my place, have you? Been inside today?" She hoped she didn't sound accusatory. Ray was a great guy, and he'd lived here since she was a little girl. She wouldn't say she was close to him like a father, but he had filled some dad roles for her—like checking out a leaky faucet or fixing her dryer.

He frowned. "I haven't been in your house. I have no reason to go in. And I haven't noticed anyone. What's going on?"

"You wouldn't happen to want to take off your gardening gloves, would you?" Duke asked. "Let me see your right hand."

Brigitte's insides curled up. Ray was not the attacker.

Ray looked from Duke to Brigitte and back to Duke. "I don't know what's going on, but no, no, I don't think I'll be removing my gloves. And furthermore, you are welcome to have your keys back, Brigitte. I don't intrude in people's homes." A flash of disappointment dimmed his eyes.

"No, no, I don't want them back. I'm sorry, Ray." She tried to explain, but he shook his head and left her with no excuses and no more apologies. Turning to Duke, she scowled. "It's not Ray. And you could have been subtler. Not so accusatory. He's my neighbor and a friend."

Duke pulled into her driveway, his cheek twitched. "You're right. I'm sorry. I let my emotions rule. I'm actually a much better agent than that."

She huffed and exited the car, picking up the bag of lunch as she entered the house. Not that she had an appetite anymore. "I would think you should be. Ray'll never step foot in my house again, and what if my pilot light goes out or something?"

Duke had the nerve to chuckle.

She rambled when she was nervous or feeling awkward, but he already knew that. "Well, it could. And I don't know how start a pilot light. Truth be told, I'm not sure I even have one or know what a pilot light goes to." She tossed her hands in the air and marched into the kitchen, dropping the lunch sack on the table. "But if I did have one and it went out, what would I do?"

Duke entered her personal space. "A pilot light goes to your furnace." He laid a hand on her shoulder. "And you are smart, resourceful and would figure it out."

"I am, and I'd use my smart thinking to call Ray, who is a resource, and now he thinks I think he did something criminal. And it's all your fault. What do you have to say for yourself?"

He cocked his head and held her gaze until she almost squirmed. "You like to pick fights when you're scared. Noted. And you prattle when you're nervous. I've already noted that."

"I do not pick fights when I'm scared. Take that back."

"No? You sure?" He grinned and pointed to his chest. "I don't really like to fight, and most assuredly not over trivial things or hypothetical situations, and when I'm nervous, I don't talk at all. When I'm scared, I fix things." He strode to the kitchen door leading to the garage.

"I'm not scared." Except she was.

"Well, come on."

What on earth? She followed him into the garage, and he walked to the water heater and knelt. "What are you doing?"

"Since your oven is electric, you have no pilot light. But you do have one with this. See this sticker? If your water won't heat up and this little light is off, call the number on the sticker. And they'll come light it. And you might have one on your furnace, and there'll be a sticker on that, too. Call the number. Fixed."

She couldn't figure this man out. "Are you being a smart aleck?"

He laughed. "No."

"'Cause you sound like it."

"Are you picking a fight? 'Cause you sound like it." He stood and dusted his hands on his thighs.

"No." *Maybe a little*.

"You hungry?"

She crossed her arms, feeling like a total heel. "No."

"You pout when you're embarrassed. Noted." He strode back into the kitchen.

She did not like working with a profiler. He was going to notice and profile her every nuance and tic.

What if he profiled the fact that she might be crushing on him? A whole new kind of fear crept over her skin, and she debated going back inside, but a killer had come after her for the third time now. She was no cat. No nine lives. That meant they had to stop him.

Fast.

\* \* \*

Duke stared at the coffeepot. Definitely not what Brigitte needed after a near-fatal attack. Again. This killer wasn't playing around. Wasn't stalking her or waiting. The killer felt an urgency to take Brigitte down and out. Rage? Focused retribution, or was it something Duke couldn't put his finger on? He'd worn a mask, but Brigitte had drawn his eyes. They were dark and glazed with malice. She'd captured that well. Too well. The sketches had given him shivers.

Now, she sat on the floor in her living room going through the photo albums, because she said it soothed her. He couldn't imagine the loss she'd suffered in the past few years, and having to watch a loved one shrink before her eyes…no, he couldn't begin to imagine that kind of pain. But he did know pain and loss. So he left her to thumb through old memories of happier times while he riffled through her kitchen cabinets.

He found a box of herbal tea and filled the kettle with water. Tea was a much better choice than caffeine. Brigitte was chatty enough, but he found it endearing and flat out cute. What wasn't cute was a killer had at least cased her house. He knew where to exit and, it appeared, where to enter. That window had been messed with. He'd come inside and left the front door unlocked on purpose. Why?

False sense of security? He'd know she would be on edge. Then to see that would terrify her. They'd cleared the house thoroughly. He couldn't have been hiding inside. But maybe he'd been perched outside the window on the lattice, then he'd crawled back in after she had settled in or went up into the attic. He wouldn't know Duke was returning.

He'd made his move, and Duke had interrupted him. He'd gone straight out the window and down the lattice when Brigitte had descended the stairs. Either he'd hidden in a yard or had a car stashed—or both.

Duke hadn't taken the neighbor Ray off the hook, but he trusted Brigitte's judgment. She was right; he'd put Ray on alert with his line of questioning. If he was the killer, then Duke had revealed too much too soon.

The kettle whistled, and he poured the boiling water over the herbal tea bag. Mint and something fruity wafted on the steam, which reminded him of early mornings. The killer was obsessed with them—with sunrises, which might have something to do with his past. Unable to watch it with whom he wanted, he used victims as surrogates. It was one sick idea, but that was the road Duke had to go down in his job.

He removed the tea bag and carried the cup into the living room. Brigitte glanced up then did a double take.

"You made me tea."

"You didn't hear the whistle?"

"No, actually. I was lost in the past. I wish you could have known my dad when all his faculties were present. He was such fun. And a romantic. He'd whisk my mom off the couch to dance to nothing but the music in his head."

"She must have loved that."

Her lips turned south. "I don't think she did. My mom was…here but not. My dad picked up a lot of the slack. I think he may have even taken up painting for me once. When I was about ten…maybe a little younger. That brooch I saw, it brought back memories of me thinking my dad had been painting." She shrugged. "I don't know. It was weird."

Duke handed her the hot mug of tea, and she accepted and thanked him. "Traumatic situations can trigger memories we've suppressed. I imagine that's what happened."

"Why would I suppress my dad painting?"

"How did the memory make you feel?"

She sipped her tea. "Scared. Or maybe I was already scared."

"When you think back on it now that you're not afraid, how does it make you feel?"

Setting the cup on the coffee table, she blew out a heavy breath. "Confused and still frightened."

Then her memory may not be one of happier times after all. Maybe she had something locked in there that she didn't want to remember, but another traumatic experience cracked open the beginning of a memory. "The brooch triggered it?"

She nodded. "When I saw the ruby gem. I remembered Dad painting—his hands had red paint on them."

Duke kept silent. Better not to give her any ideas that might create a false memory. But that might not have been paint at all. "The brooch puzzles me, too. How about we describe it to Kayla's family and see if it sounds familiar? And we can retrace her steps, talk to friends. See where it leads."

"Let me change and we can get to it."

In twenty minutes, they were at the two-story flower shop where Kayla worked below and rented out the apartment upstairs. The place was empty and smelled like a funeral home, with all the perfume and premade arrangements. Duke had never been fond of floral shops. Or funeral homes.

They were met by the manager, Helen Fleetwood.

She was in her late thirties. Hair blond and bigger than her waist and crystal blue eyes. "Well, it's only a day late and a dollar short." She shook her head and grabbed a tissue, blotting her eyes.

"How's that, ma'am?" Duke asked.

"Kayla was positive that she was being stalked. That someone had been in her home prior to her death. I told her to go to the police, but she said they wouldn't do anything. She had no solid proof." She sniffed. "Now it's too late."

Duke's gut twisted. Brigitte's home hadn't been turned upside down, either, but she had been messed with. Maybe the killer toyed with all his victims before actually killing them. Getting into their homes. Following them. "Can you tell us how long this had been happening to Kayla?"

"She said about a month, but it was only a week before she died that she confided in me." Helen blew her nose and tossed the pink tissue in the trash by the counter.

Kayla had been murdered before sunrise, but only hours before. Which meant the killer had her in his clutches and alive sometime in the middle of the night or predawn hours. "Did she work over the weekend?"

"We're closed on Sundays. But she worked Saturday. Eight to four. I left at noon and she closed up, then worked on arrangements until about seven. I know that much, because she called me about that time to let me know she'd done everything and we could both enjoy our Sunday."

So the killer had from seven on Saturday evening until twilight on Monday morning to abduct her, assault her and strangle her. They needed someone who had seen or heard from her over the weekend to help them home in on when she was taken. And where. Could have been her apartment upstairs or elsewhere. According to the Los Artes police report, there had been no signs of struggle, which could allude to the fact that she might have known her killer. Because Kayla lived in Los Artes but was found in Gran Valle, the two neighboring police departments were working in tandem.

"Had she talked about anyone? A boyfriend. Friends. Gone to any new places?" Brigitte asked.

"No." Helen's eyes suddenly widened, and she nodded. "Yes. She took an art class in El Paso. It was Saturday mornings for eight weeks. Ended Saturday before last. That's why she worked all day this past Saturday."

"Where in El Paso?"

"The Hope Community Center. A friend of hers who lives in El Paso told her about it. The guy who taught it used to teach art at Gran Valle Community."

"David Hyatt?" Brigitte asked.

"Yes! That's him."

Brigitte turned to Duke. "David taught watercolors at Gran Valle. He moved to El Paso a year ago. Does some courses and trainings on the side. I've helped him before, when he did a watercolor class for an assisted living center in El Paso. He could be a big help."

"We'll call him after we take a look at Kayla's apartment upstairs."

"Go on up." Helen touched the hollow on her throat. "I just can't believe she's gone."

Brigitte put her arms around her. "We're going to do everything we can to find who did this. You've been such a big help. One last thing." She described the brooch. "Do you know if she wore one like that?"

Helen cocked her head. "Can't say I remember her wearing something like that. Kayla didn't wear too much costume jewelry. Always her amethyst necklace. Her father gave it to her when she was fifteen, and he died tragically a few months later. She wore it faithfully, and an amethyst ring on her right middle finger. It was an heirloom from her grandmother and her birthstone."

Duke didn't remember seeing a necklace on Kayla's body in the photos, but he did remember a ring. Would the killer have taken two items of jewelry?

They went upstairs to her meticulously clean apartment, minus what the police had left behind, like print dust. "You remember a necklace on the vic?" he asked.

"No. Just the brooch beside her."

"I'd like to go back to my notes and see if any of the other victims had been involved in art, even if it was hobby classes. You're an artist. Kayla took art classes. If we could find a few more connections, we might be able to track a lead."

"I agree." Brigitte and Duke slipped on gloves and nosed through Kayla's belongings, opening cupboards and closets. Who was Kayla Lowe? "Have you gotten her phone records yet? See if she called someone or if a particular number called her often? Maybe this guy did more than stalk and get into her apartment?"

"It's possible. I'll have them sent over to us." Duke spotted a floral arrangement on the kitchen counter. No card attached. He turned and bumped the vase then righted it and noticed something in a sliver of space between the oven and the counter. His fingers wouldn't fit. He opened a couple of drawers until he found a butter knife. Carefully, he used the knife to slide the object from the space. It tumbled to the floor. A blank

"I elbowed him. Think I broke his nose. He ran after that—didn't even take his stuff with him." She gestured over to the counter.

As proud as he was that she'd successfully defended herself, the pride didn't ease his panic at the sight of the shower curtain and clothesline. She could take care of herself, but that didn't make it any easier to accept that she'd been targeted. He didn't know if this had anything to do with the case—but the shower curtain and line the assailant left behind suggested it did. They might have just caught a break, but at what expense? He wouldn't risk Cecile's life even to catch a serial killer.

She rubbed her arms and he spotted goose bumps on them. "I'd better go clean up before someone sees me like this."

She walked across the hall into the bathroom and shut the door. He checked the rest of the windows and then double-checked the locks. The house was as secure as he could make it for now—but that wasn't nearly as secure as he'd like.

The presence of the shower curtain and clothesline seemed to suggest she'd been deliberately targeted. Josh prayed the blood evidence would provide them with a DNA match, but that would be days, maybe weeks, away. They couldn't wait that long. He'd already lost Haley to a killer.

He couldn't lose Cecile, too.

*Don't miss*
Texas Buried Secrets *by Virginia Vaughan,*
*available August 2022 wherever*
*Love Inspired Suspense books and ebooks are sold.*

LoveInspired.com

Within ten minutes of her call, Cecile's home and property
were surrounded by sheriff's deputies and forensics
personnel.

Josh was one of the first to arrive. He found her on the
couch. He'd never seen her look so fragile before. It worried
him—even though her demeanor changed the moment she
saw him. She slipped on her mask of confidence as she stood
to face him.

"What happened?" He resisted the urge to pull her into
an embrace. Not only would that be unprofessional, but he
didn't want to blur the lines between them any more than
they already were.

"A man broke into my house." She explained hearing the
glass breaking and then finding the broken glass and dirty
shoe print. "He grabbed me from behind and knocked my
gun out of my hands, but I managed to fight him off."

Josh glanced at the trail of blood. She'd connected with
the assailant.

Kipling's son. He was in his early fifties, thick hair with more salt than pepper. Leaning on his walker, he grinned. "Mom's asleep," he said.

Brigitte felt a twinge of disappointment. She'd hoped to slip in for a few moments after visiting Dad. "Bummer. How is she tonight?"

"You know Mom. Never complains much. I could tell she was pretty tired, though. I worry about her." His expression softened, and he patted her shoulder, lifting one hand on his walker. Guess his neuropathy was in bad form tonight. A car accident had left him with an injury that resulted in permanent nerve damage in his legs and feet. Sometimes he used a cane, sometimes a walker, and when it was really bad and he couldn't feel his feet at all, he used a scooter. But he didn't complain much, either. Took after his mom. "I'm glad you're here for her. It does her good. She thinks of you as family."

"I think of her as family, too. And as I've said before, if you need anything at all, please let me know. I'd be happy to help you."

"I know. I'm still active and as fit as one can be. Work these ole arms out daily." He flexed, and Brigitte snickered. "Besides, keeping company with Mom is the best thing you can do. I keep saying when I retire I'll move back home to be closer. Maybe I should retire early."

El Paso wasn't terribly far, but it was a long drive if one worked late.

"I just feel old, you know? And guilty for wanting to keep working and feeling useful." He waved off his words. "Go see your old man."

Brigitte recognized the cue. Vance was done feel-

ing sorry for himself and dumping on Brigitte. "I will. Take care."

"Be back this weekend unless she needs anything. If so, call me." Vance scooted his walker and Brigitte tried not to wince at his struggle. She bustled to Dad's room and slowly inched open the door.

He rested in his recliner with the remote in his hand. His blond hair was disheveled, and his reading glasses hung around his neck on a chain. She'd purchased those when he kept losing them more than he ought to. It was the first clue something beyond absentmindedness was at play.

Dad glanced up and grinned. "Mary!"

Brigitte's heart sank. More and more he forgot who she was, living in the past and oblivious to the present. "Hi, Dad. It's Brigitte. Not Mary."

"Where's Mary?"

"Not here. Can I sit with you?"

"Of course."

She took the chair next to him and made small talk. What did he eat? Was it good? Was he cold? Did he need anything?

Finally, when his eyes drooped, she stood. "I'm going to go now, Dad."

He glanced up again, and lucidness flooded his eyes. "Brig. Baby. It's so good to see you."

Tears stung the backs of her eyes. It was so good to be seen. To be known by her father. "Hi, Daddy."

"How long have you been here?"

"Not long," she fibbed. It had been over an hour; the nurses gave her some leeway, likely because of her profession.

"How's the painting?"

"Good. I'm working on a new morning desert scene. A lot of pink hues." She smiled and returned to the chair, soaking up all she could while it lasted.

"That's so nice. You'll have to show it to me when you finish. You have such a lovely gift."

"Thank you. Dad, did you ever paint?"

"Me?" He grinned. "No. I left that to the real artist—you. Knew you had it in you from the time you were two. I finger painted occasionally with you. Does that count?"

No. But she'd seen red paint on his hands, and he'd said he had been painting. Had he forgotten or had he lied back then? "Sure."

"You seeing anyone new?" he asked and took her hand in his. Warm. Safe. Intended.

"No." But she'd met someone. "I'm working with a new guy, though. He's really…" *Incredible.* "…smart. Dedicated to his job. Kind."

Dad's eyebrows shot north. "Sounds like you more than work with him."

"No. It's not like that." He'd all but said he'd been absent though present in his marriage, and she had all her baggage—not to mention he was only here for a case. "I barely know him." Crazy how comfortable she felt around him, though.

"I knew your mom all my life. But when I knew I loved her, it was like seeing her for the first time." He grinned, his eyes lit up and full of love for Mom. "We got married at the justice of the peace. I don't know if I'd ever been so happy. To be your mom's husband. To know she was mine till death do us part."

She wanted that kind of love. Love that endured, hoped the best, was sacrificial. But if her own dad had

put in the effort with no return, nothing was guaranteed, and she hated the heartbreak it had caused him. The sadness. That same alone feeling she felt.

"Where's Mary?" he asked, his brow knitted and confusion clouding his once-clear eyes.

"She's not here right now." The moment was gone, but she'd remember it. Hang on to it in case another one never came. "She loves you, though. So do I."

"I've missed you, Mary," he said and took Brigitte's hand. "I'm so sorry."

Apologizing again. "What are you sorry for?" Brigitte asked.

Dad closed his eyes, his face scrunched as he shook his head. "I should have been there."

"Been where, Dad?"

He opened his eyes. "I'm tired."

Brigitte tucked his blanket around him and kissed his forehead. "Night, Dad," she whispered and slipped from his room, quietly closing his door and slipping down the hall past Mrs. Kipling's room and back the way she came.

She exited into the balmy night and empty parking lot. Chill bumps spiked along her arms and hairs rose on her neck. Pausing, she scanned the lot. When her eyes had fully adjusted to the darkness, she proceeded toward her Jeep, watching carefully and cautiously.

Her car was near the edge of the park, which wasn't far but felt a football field away. Adrenaline raced, and she kept her eyes peeled. Finally she reached the Jeep and grabbed the keys from her purse. As she pressed her fob and the locks clicked and bolted upward, a sense of relief washed over her. She opened the door just as a man leaped from his crouched position behind the car.

Brigitte braced herself, tossed her purse inside the Jeep and swung her fist, connecting with his hard jaw. He winced but didn't slow.

He shoved her against the Jeep, snaking a strong arm around her throat, then he squeezed with insurmountable force.

Brigitte shoved her hand into her pocket and drew her phone as she battled with the beast of a man cutting off her airway. Her eyes watered and her throat felt like it might explode from the pressure, but as her phone unlocked at her touch, she hoped she hit the last number dialed before it clattered to the asphalt.

Hotel rooms were getting old, the older Duke got. Impersonal. Empty. Like his life had been since Deena left—and if he was honest, even before. While he'd returned to his faith and church, he continued to feel disconnected. He had no opportunity to build relationships, because his job often had him traveling and in the field. At least he didn't have to leave Christ when he left town—He was always with Duke.

The day had been long and exhausting but not unpleasant like it sometimes could be. Brigitte brought color to the moments. It wasn't the fact she was a painter. She was simply fresh and unique. He'd dropped her off and felt a tinge of disappointment having to retreat to this square box with a bed and bathroom. But he'd found some solace in the word as he'd read Proverbs 4.

*"But the path of the just is as the shining light..."*

He'd prayed their path would shine light and help them bring justice.

Duke's phone rang. Brigitte. His heart kicked up a

notch, and he frowned at the visceral reaction but answered. His mouth opened, but the words froze on his tongue as Brigitte's garbled voice reached his ears.

"Brigitte!" he called, and his mind raced as panic started to seep into his bloodstream, racing hot and cold at once. Where would she be?

Sunny Days assisted living.

"Brig, hang on. I'm coming!" He snatched his gun and keys and blew out the hotel room door, sprinting to his rental car then slamming the pedal to the floor to get to her, every second of her garbled cries in a battle for her life sending him over the edge.

"Just hang on," he hollered. "Fight!" He had no idea if she could hear him or not. But he prayed his words reached her ears and gave her hope and motive to keep fighting. He prayed God would intervene.

The town wasn't large, and the assisted living center wasn't far from his hotel. He screeched into the empty visitor parking lot and spotted a masked dark figure running. Duke jumped from his car, leaving his keys inside, and followed. Up ahead Brigitte was sprinting toward the side street between the living center and the eye doctor's office.

The perp took a hard left near the cardiology center. Duke continued to give chase, hollering for him to freeze, but that was always a pointless plea. They never did. As Duke rounded the eye clinic, he lost sight of the assailant, aware of the irony.

He couldn't see Brigitte either.

"Brig!" Chest heaving, Duke surveyed the area, but the dark night was like a veil concealing the wicked. He kicked at the asphalt and jogged around the build-

ing, gun and Maglite in hand as he hunted for the hunter who'd made Brigitte his prey.

Brigitte rounded the corner facing the assisted living center's north entrance. She was breathing heavy and raking a hand through her long dark hair that was disheveled from the fight.

He closed the distance between them and instinctively smoothed her locks and ran his thumb across her cheek. "You did good, Brig." *Brig.* It had popped out his mouth on the phone with her. Like he'd been calling her that for decades. Natural. Easy. He noticed faint bruising around her tender neck. "Do you need medical attention?"

She shook her head. "No. My throat's a little raw and sore, but other than that I'm okay. I wasn't sure if the call had gone through or not. But I thought I heard your voice. Heard you tell me to hang on and that you were coming."

"I did," he said softly. "I heard you."

Her eyes filled with moisture. "It's good to be heard." She half smiled and held his gaze. The emotions of gratitude, thankfulness and what looked like a good dose of longing connected with his heart.

*Oh boy.* This was thorny territory.

He let his hand drop from her face and stuffed it into his pocket. "I'm sorry I didn't get him."

"He's slippery. And strong." She shuddered, and he almost drew her into his arms. Almost. He was feeling too much too quick and could barely keep up with the strange pull toward her. Whatever was awakening needed to take a few pain pills and go back to bed. Because there was an unmistakable ache in his chest, and he couldn't pinpoint the reason.

Didn't even want to try.

"He's keeping tabs on you. You'll need to make sure to be more careful, keep your eyes on that rearview mirror. I'll follow you home. Make sure you get in safely."

"Make me some tea?" she said through a smirk that flipped his insides upside down.

"I could do that." He waited for her to get inside her Jeep, then tailed her home. She pulled into the garage, and he followed her inside. She hit the button by the kitchen door, and the garage door lowered.

Inside the kitchen he inhaled the sweet scent of Brigitte and the lingering aroma of coffee—or maybe it was a candle. The light above the stove was on. She entered the living room, where she flipped on a lamp by the sofa.

"I was kidding about the tea," she said, and he noticed her pink cheeks.

"I wasn't." He headed into the kitchen, filled the kettle with water and turned on the burner, then returned to the living room. "Did he say anything to you when he attacked you? What exactly happened?"

Brigitte plopped on the sofa and slid her shoes off, then covered her middle with a navy throw pillow. Guarding herself. Usually it was a show of insecurity and a need for safety and comfort. He studied her posture.

On the edge of the couch, feet touching the floor. Her fingers running along the outer ribbing of the pillow. She was still shaken, not ready to relax. Not quite feeling safe. But her face was stoic. Not even a hint of fear or concern. She'd learned that from the job.

She told him everything about the attack and how it happened. "He didn't say a word. His eyes looked dark,

but I can't be sure if they were brown, hazel or even dark blue. I know they were cold. He had no emotion. He was there for a job and to get the job done. Unlike the way he approached the other victims."

Duke leaned against the wall, knowing the teakettle would whistle any minute. "No, he abducts them, assaults them and then stages them in the desert. Takes his time. What happened to you tonight, in the attack in the mechanic's garage and here is different. You appear to be his highest priority now."

"I feel so important," she deadpanned, and he laughed. The kettle whistle blew, and she startled.

"You're safe now. I'm not going to let anything happen to you." And he wouldn't. He couldn't. He made the same herbal tea from earlier and brought it to her. She'd finally drawn her feet up under her as she settled on the couch, but the pillow was still a barrier between her and whatever might come near her.

Good. He kinda wanted to come nearer. The pillow reminded him he wasn't emotionally available. She received the tea and cradled it between her palms, the steam pluming and filling the room with its minty, fruity scent.

They sat in comfortable silence as she sipped her tea and relaxed. Finally, the pillow fell to her lap and then to side of the couch, and her eyes closed.

A crack of thunder jolted her from her peaceful moment and from Duke's enjoyment of watching her, studying her face—the high bone structure. The softness, the way her eyelashes fanned out as her eyes closed and her full lips had a perfect cupid's bow.

"I didn't know it was gonna storm."

"Is that a metaphor?"

"Maybe." She chuckled. "But truly, I just wanted to let off some steam, relax, work through stress by painting that morning. I had no idea what I'd find. As if I already don't have enough to deal with."

"I'm sorry," he murmured as a flash of lightning lit up the sky and another crack of thunder unleashed. "You want to talk about it?"

"Yes. And no. My dad remembered me tonight. For a little while, and it felt so…*good* isn't the right word. So…safe. Like for just a minute I wasn't all alone and unknown." She sipped her tea then sighed. "Does that sound ridiculous?"

"No. Everyone wants to be known." And loved anyway. Even Duke. But his flaws and weaknesses had been used as nails to bury him in a coffin of brokenness. Deena had blamed so much on him, and she'd been right about most of it. But she wasn't innocent in it, either. And she hadn't wanted to fight through the flaws and work on them together.

"When I was little, we'd go to the lake, and I remember lying on a blanket gazing at clouds. I'd see all sorts of shapes and objects. I'd point them out, but Mom and Dad could never see them. I think that's when I realized I might see the world differently. And it was the first time I felt alone. I couldn't have been more than eight or nine. What was supposed to be a lovely day wasn't. I mean, what kid feels alone because a parent can't see a unicorn in a cloud?"

She half laughed, but he felt the sorrow and confusion. "Now I think it was more than that. I felt the tension in my parents' marriage. The aloofness of my mother and my dad trying to make up for it—which I appreciated, but looking back, I felt that. Nothing I did,

no picture I drew or page I colored seemed to draw my mom closer. I mean, I know she loved me. I don't doubt that, but it was sporadically shown."

"Being misunderstood at any age makes an impact. It's rough when someone won't see what you see—or even try. Frustrating. When I found out my ex cheated on me, I was surprised. I didn't realize anything was wrong, but looking back I know there was. My being gone at work all the time was being distant to her. But to me, I was providing for us. I've never been great at articulating my feelings." He was doing it rather easily now, though. That was something to wonder about—or not. "I get feeling alone and misunderstood." He shrugged one shoulder. "I've never even tried to see something in a cloud." His parents had never encouraged daydreaming, and he'd always been a practical kid and man.

"Never?"

"Nope."

"You should try. Then tell me what you saw."

"Maybe I'll do that." He stood. "It's late. I should be going."

Brigitte nodded. "Or…" She ran her teeth across her bottom lip. "You could stay. I have a guest room upstairs."

He studied her shaky hands and fearful eyes. "All right," he murmured, and it dawned on him he'd never be able to tell this woman no.

And that terrified him.

# FIVE

Brigitte awoke to the sun peeping through her window. It had stormed most of the night, but she'd felt safer knowing that Duke was in the house. She checked her cell phone. Nearly nine o'clock. Was he even still here? Duke seemed like an early-to-rise, early-to-work kind of man. She threw back her rumpled covers and made a beeline to her bathroom, where she splashed water on her face, pulled her hair into a ponytail and brushed her teeth.

She sniffed.

Was that coffee…and bacon? She quickly dressed in a pair of jeans and a T-shirt and hurried downstairs to find Duke making himself at home in her kitchen. His dress shirt was rumpled and rolled to his elbows and his hair was a little disheveled, but it suited him.

When he saw her, he grinned. "I had a feeling the smell of caffeine and bacon would wake you. I hope you don't mind me taking the liberty. I ran out to that corner store and grabbed eggs and bacon."

She shook her head and poured a steaming cup of coffee, adding a splash of cream and spoonful of sugar. "Not at all. You should have woken me earlier."

"You needed the rest. Long day." He turned off the burner and piled the bacon onto paper towels covering a plate, then poured out some grease and dumped in the eggs he'd scrambled into a bowl.

"I'm usually in such a hurry I microwave bacon and throw it on toast. Yay for eggs."

He chuckled. "I'd say microwaved bacon is no way to eat bacon, but it's bacon, so other than raw it's a win." He used the spatula to stir the eggs and added salt and pepper while Brigitte sipped her coffee at the table. He plated the fare and tossed on a piece of toast.

"This looks and smells amazing." She indulged in a bite and closed her eyes. "You like to cook? You could totally beat Bobby Flay with these eggs."

He smirked. "Bobby Flay an old boyfriend?"

Brigitte nearly choked on her coffee. "Uh, no. He's a big-time chef with a show where lesser-known chefs try to beat him with their signature dishes."

"Ah. And do they?"

"Occasionally." She scooped up another forkful of eggs.

"I learned to cook because I had to eat. I don't mind it. I wouldn't call myself a chef—even amateur."

"Well, you should." She crunched into her wheat toast. "What's the plan for today?"

"Time to talk to David Hyatt. See if he can be of any help regarding Kayla Lowe. If he's in El Paso, we need to make the trip. Plus, I promised friends I'd come by and see them. Twofer. Would you be interested in the side thing?"

He wanted her to come with him to meet his friends? No. She was just with him and he was trying to kill two

birds with one stone. "I don't want to impose. I can call David and you can go see friends."

"It's not an imposition. Besides, Chelsey can give us some good insight. She was an analyst—"

"Chelsey Banks? The Outlaw killer came after her. I saw her on TV with the Texas Ranger." *Whoa.* "I didn't realize she wasn't with the unit anymore or that she was in El Paso."

Duke nodded. "She left the BAU to take a job with the Texas Rangers doing consultant work. She just married a couple of months ago—to the Texas Ranger."

"Oh. Wow. Okay, yeah, that sounds intriguing."

Duke grinned. "Marrying a Ranger?"

"Hearing that story." She snickered. "I need to go by and see Dad first. I can do that while—"

"I think I'll go along this time." He raised his eyebrows. "I don't have to go in or anything—just want to be some backup."

"I'm a fan of backup." She carried her plate to the sink and rinsed it, then placed it in the dishwasher. "I'm gonna go get ready."

"Me, too. I'll be back in about an hour. That work?"

"Yep."

Brigitte walked him to the door. The sky was overcast, and her yard was damp from the rain. A few limbs had fallen. Duke stepped out and glanced at the side yard, then frowned and tromped over. She followed him into the squishy yard.

Duke stood near the window that looked into the living room.

"What is it, Duke?" Brigitte tiptoed over and followed his gaze to the soggy ground. Two large boot impressions had been made in the mud where some-

one must have been standing, peeping inside. Brigitte's heart lurched into her throat.

"He was here. Last night. After the rain. During. Not sure. Or early this morning, before daylight, maybe." Duke glanced to the left and followed the prints, which stayed close to the house and led into the backyard then around to the other side, as if whoever made them had been looking for ways to sneak in or calculate a plan to return.

Icy fear pelted Brigitte's heart, and the thought of being here alone again turned her stomach. "We need to get someone out here to do shoe impressions. Looks like heavy work boots." Focusing on the job and what needed done would keep her mind off the fact that while she'd slept a killer had slunk around her home. The thunder and heavy rain would have muffled any noise of a prowler.

Brigitte called the Los Artes police and made the report and the call for a crime tech to come out.

Duke's eyes narrowed, and his right cheek pulsed. He huffed, hands on his hips as he turned her direction. "Brigitte, I don't like the idea of you being here alone. Especially at night."

"Would you like a warmer welcome? Here it is. Wanna stay here instead of your hotel room?" Hope swelled in her chest. She didn't want to be alone, and she didn't want to have to pack up and stay in a hotel. Besides, she couldn't afford one. Between medical bills and Dad's monthly fee at Sunny Days, it was eating up what Dad had saved and putting a good dent in her own paycheck. Thankfully, she was making a fairly decent side amount by selling paintings.

Duke chuckled. "If it won't make you feel uncom-

fortable or ruin your reputation with the neighbors. Some strange man taking up homestead."

The fact he thought about her reputation and what neighbors might say touched her deeply. "Los Artes is a small town, and by now everyone knows the Sunrise killer has tried to take me out more than once and that a big FBI agent is in town. I think our integrity is safe. But I do appreciate you thinking of it."

He nodded once, clearly uneasy with the compliment. About fifteen minutes later, a car pulled into the drive. They came around front to see Taylor Oriole and his crime scene kit exiting his car. "Hey, Brig. Things aren't really going good for you, are they?"

"Understatement, Taylor." She introduced Duke to Taylor and then told him where he'd find the shoe imprints. They left him to his job, and she ran inside to collect her things then returned outside.

Ray was walking his black Lab. "Brigitte," he said coolly. Guess he hadn't gotten over the accusation.

"Hey, Ray."

Ray glared at Duke, then noticed the car and the guy by the side of the house. "What's going on?"

"Prowler," Duke said.

"In this neighborhood?" He shook his head and heaved a sigh. "If you need anything, let me know, Brigitte. Hope you catch this guy."

"Me, too. Thanks, Ray." Looked like her apology had been accepted.

They slid in to Duke's rental car as Ray continued his walk with Midnight, his Lab.

Duke watched him walk but said nothing. Clearly, he was still suspicious. Whatever. It wasn't Ray.

"I'm glad we're going to El Paso. I could use a break from this." She redirected his attention.

"I tend to agree, even if we are still working. Do you need anything before we stop by your dad's?"

"Nope. All set."

Hopefully, the remainder of the day would be Sunrise killer–free, but the apprehensive feeling and cold dread knotted in her gut said things were far from over.

In fact, they might just be beginning.

Duke parked on the side street near a small café where David Hyatt had agreed to meet him and Brigitte. It was a little past lunchtime, but they were both hungry, so a public place made sense. Brigitte hadn't been very chatty on the drive. The morning hadn't gone well with her father. He'd had an episode, as Brigitte called them. Agitated and disoriented—calling her Mary or asking where Mary was, but with violence. He'd taken a few swings in order to get out to find Mary.

Duke wished there was something he could say or do to make it better, but words wouldn't suffice, so he'd remained quiet, giving her space and time to think through the morning while he'd enjoyed the Texas desert and scenery as they'd driven farther south.

"Sorry I've been so sullen," Brigitte said as she opened her car door.

"No need to apologize." He locked the doors with the fob and they strolled into the little café, the smells of Mexican spices hitting his senses and sending his stomach into a rumble.

Brigitte waved, and a man in the back booth stood and grinned. Dressed in business casual, hair thick and messy on his head and wearing black-framed glasses,

the man must be David Hyatt. He was older than Duke had originally assumed.

Duke followed Brigitte to the booth and stood quietly as she hugged the man and made pleasantries, then she introduced him to David.

Duke observed David's posture. Leaning toward Brigitte, eyes dilated and a few rapid blinks. His hand still resting on her arm in a subtle way one would interpret as casual.

If one wasn't trained to study behavior to build profiles.

Hyatt was attracted, even interested in Brigitte, but Duke wasn't sure if it was Brigitte as a person or simply David enjoying and wanting to pursue pretty women. Brigitte fit that bill easily in Duke's opinion.

Brigitte slid into the dark red booth with a few squeaks and Duke sat beside her; David slid into the other side but far enough over to be directly in front of Brigitte. No middle of the booth. No parallel to Duke.

"Now, how can I be of help to you, Brigitte?" David signaled a server to attend to their needs. Polite, but something simmered underneath it, as if he was entitled to her service in a way that was unnerving. "You said it was about a student of mine involved in a present case."

The server approached and took Duke and Brigitte's drink orders. David had already ordered a coffee and water. They both asked for water, no lemon, and accepted menus.

"It is."

"It must be serious if you're bringing along the FBI." David tossed Duke a closed-lip smile.

"We hope to ask you a few questions about Kayla Lowe."

"Kayla!" David's eyes lit up, then he suddenly sobered and leaned forward. "Kayla died?"

Brigitte informed him of what had happened, leaving out the fact she herself had been the one to interrupt the Sunrise Serial Killer.

David's mouth turned down, and he slowly sipped his water. "She was talented. It was raw and needed honing, but she was good. I'm sorry to hear this. How can I help?"

The server returned for their orders. Duke chose the enchiladas, and Brigitte ordered a steak-and-chicken quesadilla. David ordered the steak fajitas. After the server left them to their privacy, Brigitte leaned in. "Tell us about the class she was in and the students. Any males thirty-five to forty-five?"

Based on the first crime, the profile depicted a white male in his early thirties. That was eighteen years ago, making him mid- to late forties, or with some wiggle room if he started killing earlier.

"I'd have to check. I can email my admin assistant." He picked up his phone and sent a text. "Off the top of my head, I'd say most of the men were in their twenties. We had a few fifty-plus men. Maybe one or two early thirties, but it's hard to tell and I wasn't looking that hard, if you know what I mean."

Duke grinned. "Understood. Any of those men take an interest in Kayla? You ever see her talking to anyone outside of class?"

David cocked his head and frowned. "I don't know. It's possible. I know she always arrived early, and she did chitchat with a few of the young women who sat near her. I can't remember last names, but I know it was Trista, Leigh and Angel-Beth."

"Can you get us a class roster?" Brigitte asked as the sound of sizzling fajitas approached; the server placed the brightly colored plates with their entrées on the table, the smells of tomatoes, onions and peppers filling his senses.

They dug in and ate in silence a few moments, the rumbling of his stomach finally halting.

Suddenly, David paused eating. "I do remember an older man with Kayla. It was the last day of our art class, and he picked her up. He wasn't a student. I only saw her get into the car with him. I was leaving early for a doctor's appointment. It was a dark blue or black sedan. He had on sunglasses, and his hair was salt and pepper. That's all I remember. I thought it might be her father. But never thought another thing after that, and our time together was over anyway."

That might be something. "She ever talk about personal things in class to you or to others you might have overheard?"

"She liked flowers and working at the shop. She did mention she was sort of involved with someone, but I never picked up a name. Usually it was small talk overheard while they painted."

Duke wanted to talk to the friends she'd made in art class. "You have any paintings of hers?"

"No, they were allowed to keep them all after our final class. She mostly did flowers and scenery. A couple of sunrises."

"You know where she got her inspiration?"

"No. 'Fraid not."

Duke nodded and continued eating his lunch. David's phone chimed, and he checked it. "Sabrina sent

the roster to my email. I have yours, Brigitte. I'll forward it to you, if that's all right."

"Of course," she said through a bite of rice and beans.

David toyed with the straw paper, rolling it into a ball. Something was on his mind, but Duke didn't ask. He waited. Finally, David leaned forward. "Why do you think he—the Sunrise killer—leaves his victims in the desert to await the sun coming up?"

"Why do you?" Duke countered.

The other man's neck reddened, and he cleared his throat. "I'm not the FBI. But maybe—if all his victims are artists—there's something artistically related to the sunrise."

Insightful. Maybe too insightful? "You said Kayla mostly stuck to flowers. However, she'd done a couple of sunrises. Any other students paint sunrises?" That might be the reason the targets were different in age and physicality. It wasn't a specific trait that triggered the killer but what the intended victim was drawn to and painted. Like sunrises.

If the killer was prowling art classes, whether paid or free, that might be how he was selecting his prey, but Duke didn't want to give too much of his thoughts away. David was late forties, and he wasn't ruling him out as a suspect at this point. He might sit on that idea and keep it from Brigitte, too. She clearly didn't believe David could be a suspect, but he had a clear avenue to the victims. Even if he wasn't instructing classes, who was to say he wasn't attending?

"Off the top of my head, I don't recall. Sunsets, though. We had a few who painted the setting sun."

But it was the rising sun that fascinated the killer. He was infatuated by it. "Can we also get a list of proj-

ects previous artists in your class painted? Say, for the past five years." He'd also see if he could get an analyst at the BAU to do some behind-the-scenes digging on David Hyatt. Duke wanted to know if any of the previous victims were in his classes or if they could connect any of the victims to David in other ways, and if they were in classes together, Duke wanted to know what they painted. This could be a lead.

"Of course." He went to work texting again and then pocketed his phone. They finished their meals, paid the bill and he and Brigitte exited the café into the blazing sun. The storm had done nothing but bring in more heat.

"You think the killer is targeting painters of sunrises, don't you?" Brigitte fastened her seat belt and set her purse on the floorboard by her feet.

"I think it's possible. Other than gray eyes, nothing else fits. We have women in their twenties, thirties and forties as victims. Three out of five lived in Los Artes, one in Gran Valle and one in El Paso, but they were all left in various places in the desert near Gran Valle. So we can't be sure how or where he targeted them, but Los Artes is known as a hub for artists. Either way, artistry might be a good place to help us narrow down the hunting ground."

He turned the ignition, but the engine didn't roll over. Nothing but a click.

"Alternator? Battery?" Brigitte asked and fanned her face.

"No," Duke said, his stomach forming a knot. It didn't sound like either. The click was different. Like something had been locked into place. "Brigitte, get out of the car! Now!"

At the same time, they opened their doors, and as

Duke's foot hit the pavement, a deafening boom and a wave of intense heat seared his back as his feet lifted off the ground.

Did Brigitte make it out of the car?

# SIX

Brigitte landed on her side with a thud that rattled her bones. Ears ringing, disoriented and flooded with heat, she sat up and gauged the situation. She was in the car. Then Duke told her to get out. She'd immediately obeyed, based on the urgency in his deep, gravelly voice.

*Duke.*

Where was Duke? A crowd had formed; sirens blared. Someone knelt by her, asking if she was okay. She blinked, and her blurred vision cleared. David. It was David.

"I'm okay." She had no clue if she was or not, but Duke wasn't beside her. The car hood was lying several feet away in the street. Flames licked what was left, and inky smoke billowed in the air, covered the atmosphere. She coughed and shifted.

"Careful. There's glass," David said. Ignoring him, she rose.

"I need to find Duke." She swayed, dizziness zinging along the back of her head, but she pushed forward through the onlookers and around the car. Glass had been blown out and scattered like glittering diamonds on the road and sidewalks. But no buildings were on fire.

A bomb. The Sunrise killer had set a bomb. How? "Duke!" She pushed through people vying for her attention. About ten feet from the car, on the other side, a crowd had gathered and was hunching over something. Someone.

Duke.

Brigitte's body ached, especially her sides and back, but she pushed forward, weaving through the gathered people until she made her way to him. Duke lay on his back, the side of his face covered in blood and dirt and soot clinging to every inch of his clothing and skin.

"Duke!" She knelt beside him, ignoring the excruciating pain caused by simple movement, and lightly touched his cheek that wasn't caked in blood. "Can you hear me?" Panic sped through her veins, and her hands shook, her pulse racing at dangerous levels.

His eyes fluttered open, and he slowly trained them on her. "Brig. I thank God you're okay. Couldn't let you…" His eyes closed as paramedics charged onto the scene, pulling Brigitte away for her own treatment, and El Paso police officers followed as they asked questions.

Everything was a whirlwind but felt like slow-mo. By the time her ears unclogged and the ringing dimmed to a chime, she was in the hospital room with Duke after she was released. No concussion, thankfully, but she had severe bruising and several abrasions they'd cleaned and bandaged.

She'd inched down the corridor to Duke's room, thanks to a nurse helping her out with directions, and knocked on the door. Voices sounded, and she ignored politeness and went inside to see an exasperated nurse arguing with a menacing and powerful Duke Jericho.

"If I can carry on a coherent conversation with you, then I can clearly function on my own," Duke groused.

"The fact you think this conversation is wise to even have tells me you are not coherent. You have a concussion, six stitches on your head and two fractured ribs. You need monitoring and rest." The nurse was petite but persistent and no-nonsense.

Duke glanced up, his face still covered in soot and some splotches of dried blood. He sighed and hobbled over to Brigitte. "Tell her I'm fully capable of taking care of myself."

"Technically, I only just met you." She was half joking, but Brigitte was no doctor, so she didn't want to be tapped in for this fight.

"If that was your first date," the nurse said, "I'd think twice before a second." She gave her a knowing look.

"Well, it was so explosive," Brigitte teased out of sheer discomfort.

Duke chuckled. "See why I like her?"

"Yeah. Not sure why she likes you," the nurse muttered and shrugged. "I'll be back with a form, but again, both Dr. Timmin and I think it's best you have overnight care here, where we can monitor you."

"I'll note on the form you mentioned that. Repeatedly," he stressed.

She huffed and left the room.

Brigitte studied him. "She's probably right, you know?"

"Probably." He touched her cheek. "Any major injuries? How are you feeling?"

"Like a bomb went off in your car and I got caught in the cross hairs. You?"

"Right as rain. I wish I'd finished off those enchila-

das." He patted his stomach, making light of a seriously heavy situation. "Better hearing you're okay."

"I have bruised ribs and some pain meds for soreness. I have a headache, and you sound underwater still."

"Good. I thought it was just me." His sly grin gave her belly a loop-de-loop. Then he sobered. "I can't stay overnight here when a killer tried to take us both out with a stupid bomb. I need answers. I called my friend with the Texas Rangers—"

The door swung open, and in barreled a man bigger than Duke and larger than life in a Texas Ranger uniform—suit coat, dress pants, white Stetson and the Ranger medallion on his lapel. Next to him was a slender woman with golden skin, long brown hair and a worried look in her dark brown eyes.

"Were your ears burning?" Duke asked.

"How bad are you?" the man asked and surveyed Duke's face, then turned his attention on Brigitte. "You must be Officer Linsey. Tack Holliday, and this is Chelsey, former FBI profiler and my wife."

Chelsey rolled her eyes. "He just wants an excuse to say that."

"But you *were* FBI," Tack said, and Brigitte caught the playfulness in his eyes.

Chelsey huffed. "You know good and well I meant the wife part, Tackitt." She turned her attention back to Brigitte and grinned, then whispered loudly, "Don't tell him I kinda love it."

Newlywed bliss looked good on them.

"Secret's safe with me." She pointed to Duke. "They want him to stay overnight. He refused."

Tack grinned. "Of course he did. He's a prideful, stubborn man. It's what we do."

The nurse returned with the forms, and Duke scribbled his signature on the lines and tossed her a beaming smile. "Have a good one."

Duke strode from the room with confidence, but his gait was a little weak and wobbly.

"Hey, Einstein, you have no car. It got blown to bits. Exactly why are you leading the charge?" Chelsey asked.

Duke paused. "Oh, yeah."

Chelsey jiggled her keys. "We'll take you back to Los Artes. If you feel up to it, we can talk about this case. Today was a serious close call. I filled Vera in."

It *was* a close call, and Brigitte's insides were still quivering. Maybe Duke was in denial or putting on a brave front. Or concussed and unable to realize the depth of the situation—not only was the Sunrise Serial Killer after Brigitte, but he didn't mind Duke as collateral damage. In fact, future attempts might include Duke. If it wasn't for him, the killer would have had better success murdering Brigitte earlier. But with Duke hovering and now staying at Brigitte's, he wasn't making it easy on the killer.

"Why?" Duke groaned. "She'll just be worried for nothing."

"'Nothing,' says your fractured ribs and banged-up face," Tack added.

Duke remained silent but glanced at Brigitte, then slid his fingers between hers and squeezed. "Concern, yes. Worry, no. You're going to be okay," he whispered.

But would he?

"You trust me?"

She had no reason not to. "I do."

He gave a nod and winced. "Can we go by the drugstore and pick up our pain pills?"

Outside the hospital, Chelsey nodded as she hauled herself into a huge white pickup and Tack jumped in the passenger side. Brigitte and Duke clambered into the back seat. "No falling asleep on the ride. Concussions and all."

The ride back to Los Artes was mostly quiet. Brigitte and Duke were both spent and sore as all get-out. They passed through the drugstore and filled their prescriptions, then Brigitte gave Chelsey directions to her home.

Inside she turned on the light, instantly feeling better at being out of the hospital and in her own place of comfort—though it had been violated twice now. Still, it was good to be home. She slipped off her shoes.

"Nice place," Chelsey said and spotted the teakettle. "I'll make tea, and when y'all get hungry, Tack can run out and get some dinner, or if you have soup, I can throw that together."

"I appreciate it," Brigitte said. Chelsey was a total stranger, but she made herself at home in Brigitte's kitchen as Tack helped Duke ease onto the couch and tossed a blanket over him, their voices hushed. "You don't have to do all this. Really."

"Duke helped save my life not too long ago. You know that?"

Brigitte shook her head.

"The least I can do is feed y'all and help with the case. You two working well together?" she asked, but Brigitte had a feeling Chelsey Banks could see much more than the average bear and knew they were getting along just fine. It was in her tone and uplifted right

eyebrow. She reminded her of Belle from *Beauty and the Beast*.

"Yes, he's easy to work with."

Chelsey snorted. "Really? Because I find him to be as snarly and stubborn as a mule."

Brigitte's face ballooned with heat. "I don't know what to say. It's true."

"As I suspected." She put the kettle on. "Where can I find tea bags?"

Brigitte pointed to the cabinet, and Chelsey went to work getting out the tea and honey. "Duke's a private man and he's…he's been hurt. That's all I'm gonna say about that."

"I know about his divorce."

Chelsey's eyes widened. She didn't seem like a woman who was often surprised. "He told you? Wow. Well…wow."

"Why? Does he not talk about it much?"

"Never, actually." She studied Brigitte's face, then stared at the teakettle. "You can trust him and his gut. You're safe with him." The kettle whistled, and she dropped chamomile bags into two mugs, then poured the boiling water over them. "And I couldn't care less what he says—he's drinking this tea."

Brigitte followed Chelsey into the living room. Tack sat in the overstuffed chair near the sofa, and Duke had his feet on the ottoman and his head resting on the back of the sofa. Chelsey took the other chair, leaving Brigitte to sit beside Duke.

"Duke, don't go to sleep." Brigitte settled beside him, and he grunted, then tossed some of his blanket onto her lap. Sharing a blanket. Heat burned its way up the trunk of her body into her neck and cheeks.

He opened his eyes long enough to accept the tea with nothing but a turned-up nose. Chelsey handed them both pain meds. "Y'all don't be afraid to take them. We'll stand guard tonight, if you don't mind us crashing here, Brigitte. You two need rest."

Rest sounded wonderful. She was so tired. But she also wanted to clean off the grime and grit.

Tack stood. "Duke, give me the key to your hotel room, and I'll bring you fresh clothes." Duke reached into his pocket, retrieving his wallet. He handed Tack the card key.

"Actually, you can bring all my stuff. After the guy's been here twice, I was planning on staying until the case wrapped up. Safer. I was checking out later today anyway."

"I'll take care of it." Tack simply took the key. No questions asked.

"Thanks, man. 'Preciate it."

Tack nodded to Chelsey and she returned it, then he left the house.

"Drink your tea, then head to the shower, Brigitte. I'll make sure he doesn't fall into a coma or anything."

"I heard that."

"Good. I don't want any lip when I wake you every hour all night long." She grinned at Brigitte.

"What happened to rest?" Duke complained and sipped the tea. A surprised gurgle escaped his mouth. "Huh. This is pretty good."

Brigitte snickered and sipped her chamomile. "Any news on the bomb? I figured you might have inquired with the El Paso police or Texas Rangers."

Chelsey nodded. "We have. Easily made using a video online. It was set to blow on the ignition crank,

but he must have not done it right or you would have exploded in the driveway before ever leaving the house. So he's not familiar with bombs. Amateur. Probably his first one. I imagine it happened last night. It would have been too risky in daylight with people around."

"That explains the footprints. He might have been checking to make sure we were asleep before setting it." She told Chelsey about the wet prints.

"Probably so. However, the second turn of the ignition did the trick. The Rangers are using their crime lab to go over the evidence. Thankfully, bystanders weren't injured. If Duke hadn't recognized the clicking noise being off…well…we wouldn't be here having this conversation."

Brigitte shuddered and drew the covers up around her neck as she felt Duke's hand slip into hers under the blanket, clutching it and infusing warmth and comfort. She found herself leaning toward him, if only minimally, and resting her own head on the back of the couch. "I guess we need to be extra careful."

If the killer was willing to learn how to build a bomb, who knew what he might attempt next?

The bomb had frightened Duke more than he let on, and tucking Brigitte's hand into his wasn't only for her comfort—he'd needed it, too. Not knowing if she was seriously injured had made a major impact on his heart. He hadn't had time to process everything, including his feelings, but they were strong. Strong, hard and fast. Which terrified him on new levels.

He'd had the sense once at the hospital to call Chelsey. They needed more law enforcement power on this. The killer had stepped up his game and was

taking risks he hadn't before. It was good because he'd likely make a mistake but also horrifying because he'd deviated from his MO, and that made him a wild card.

Duke had no idea what he'd attempt next, but one thing was clear—his intent to kill Brigitte was fueled with rage, and now Duke was in the cross hairs. That much he didn't mind if he could keep Brigitte safe, but the profiler in him felt a check. Something was different. Off. Undefined, and that rattled him. Would the killer have that much rage and be pursuing this vendetta simply because Brigitte stumbled upon what may have been a last ritual before leaving his victim in the desert?

If so, the ritual was something the killer felt was essential to him personally. That only by this one thing would he be satiated. It wasn't just about the kill or even the hunt, but the whole that gave him a measure of satisfaction that would last him quite a length of time before another kill.

Brig had interrupted and halted it, so the killer now had a frustration he normally didn't. He was fixated on Brigitte for that interruption. Duke wasn't making it easy for him to get to her, either, therefore he'd need to be removed from the murderous equation—by any means necessary, including a bomb that he hadn't put together properly. *Thank You, God, for watching over us*.

He squeezed Brigitte's hand as she and Chelsey pinged ideas off one another. It was nice to see Chelsey's confidence back. She seemed happier since leaving Quantico, but it was more about Tack than walking away from the Bureau. Duke related to the restlessness Chelsey had experienced before leaving the BAU. Something was still missing from his life.

He never dreamed he'd ever have anything more than a simple attraction to or appreciation of a woman again, but in the past few days, that idea was being shaken loose by the fact he could not only feel a deep attraction, a possible lingering one, but a heavy emotional connection.

Did he even have the energy and ability to start over again? So many years in vain. Wasted. Failed. He was exhausted simply thinking about trying to trust again, date again, be vulnerable again. But then, he'd never truly been vulnerable with Deena. Never laid out his feelings. But he'd profiled her often—she'd hated that. Hated him not talking.

*"I don't even know you, Duke. Ten years. I thought I knew you. Thought maybe we were just growing apart and changing, but I'm not sure I ever really knew you. You don't let people inside. I needed to be needed."*

She'd been right. He hadn't admitted it at the time. He wasn't too concerned over his locked-up vulnerability when his wife had been having an affair with his best friend. That sort of took the driver's seat. But after time…when he tried to see if they could patch things up, he'd admitted he needed to be more open and sharing.

But it was too late.

"Duke, you awake?" Brigitte asked.

He opened his heavy eyes. Sleep was nipping at his consciousness, and he wanted nothing more than to give in to its pull and shut out all his thoughts. "I'm awake," he murmured. "Just tired."

And worried and confused.

"I know. Me, too. But you have a concussion."

He faintly heard a car in the drive, and the front door opened. Tack entered with Duke's suitcase and a

bag from the deli. "I tossed everything in the suitcase blindly. I don't need to see your skivvies."

Duke smiled, but even that hurt. He'd taken his pain meds and an antibiotic in case the stitches got infected. "Thanks."

"I'll roll it to the bathroom for you. There's club sandwiches and chips in the bag."

Chelsey stood. "I'll get drinks. You two can clean up while I set up our food. Duke, maybe tonight sleep on the couch so I can keep a watch on you. No point going up and down the stairs for either of us. And I can keep an eye on the house from here."

Duke grunted as he stood and slowly headed for the bathroom downstairs.

"I'll get him some pillows. I have extras in my closet." Brigitte stood with as much effort as it had taken Duke and inched toward her bedroom and bath.

After washing away grit and grime and slipping into sweats and a T-shirt, he admitted the hot water had helped the aching muscles. Chelsey had laid out the sandwiches, drinks and chips on the coffee table, and the couch was made up like a bed with a quilt and three pillows. Brigitte hadn't made it back into the living room yet.

Tack was already eating his club in the recliner, and Chelsey was on her laptop working.

"You know anything new?" Duke eased onto the couch and grabbed a sandwich. But he wasn't all that hungry, though it had been about six hours since they'd last eaten.

"I read over your notes and what you'd emailed. I'm stumped, to be honest, on why he's bent on Brigitte. If he is someone in the art community, she likely knows

and trusts him. He could easily abduct her and make her his next victim."

That thought soured his stomach, and he set the sandwich back on its wrapper.

Chelsey glanced up and studied him. Great. She was doing that thing she did. Duke was a great profiler, but Chelsey had unusual ability that was perfect for catching killers but irritating when she turned it on friends. Guess Deena was justified in her remarks about his own analysis of her.

"She's not that much younger than you, and she seems settled and responsible. Reliable. Dependable. I get no feel she's a serial dater or into wild parties." She pointed to a Bible on the coffee table with a journal beside it. "She's a person of faith. She takes care of her father, and painting is her passion. Love is a chance, no matter how old or mature a person is. If you want a second one…"

"I don't. I know you too well, so there's no point in lying. I'm attracted to her. She's strong and brave and amusing. She makes me smile. But that's as far as it goes. She's under my care and my partner right now, so her well-being matters to me." He snatched a bag of chips, opened it and crunched a few.

Chelsey shrugged. Tack remained silent. At least he had the decency to mind his own business. Or he was just too occupied with dinner to talk. "Fine. How are you feeling?"

"Tired and bombed."

Tack chuckled. "Cranky, too."

Duke ignored him as the door to Brigitte's master bedroom closed and she appeared in brightly colored loungewear. Her hair was hanging wet around her shoul-

ders, and without makeup she looked even younger than twenty-eight, but also weary and spent. "You hungry?"

"Not really, but I know I need to eat."

She sat next to him, and he inhaled her sweet, floral scent mixed with the smell of fabric softener. She reached for a sandwich and winced. Duke ignored his own stabbing pain and grabbed it, handing it to her.

"Thanks." She held his gaze a beat, then turned her attention on unwrapping the club. They ate in silence until she glanced up. "Where's your truck?"

"Oh," Tack said, "I parked on the other side of the street and down a few houses. In case he decides he wants to make a play again. He won't know anyone else is here but you and possibly Duke."

"Well played."

"I'm smart like that." He grinned, and Brigitte sighed.

"If there's no new information, I'm going to go on and go to bed. Duke, you'll be okay? Enough pillows?"

"I'll be just fine. Sleep well."

She nodded and paused then trekked down the hall to bed.

Tack stood and excused himself to a guest room upstairs while Chelsey took first watch and scribbled on a notepad, crunching ice. How was he supposed to sleep with that noise going all night? He settled on the couch and closed his eyes.

"One hour," Chelsey said.

"Yeah, yeah." They were fully loaded, aware of the killer's intentions, and Chelsey and Tack were excellent at their jobs. As he drifted into sleep, safety cocooned his heart, but his brain warned him not to drift too deep.

# SEVEN

"If art is the connection, how do victims one, three and four fit in? From everything I can gather, none of them were artists or attended art classes—at least that I can track, and quite frankly, I'm a good tracker." Duke huffed and winced as he sat at the head of the small table in the Gran Valle Police Department's conference room.

Brigitte wasn't sure how it all connected, either. But she felt every bit of that wince. Her body was stiff and tender, and that was after sleeping until eight o'clock this morning. Duke had been up when she came downstairs—she'd just missed Chelsey and Tack's exit. Duke had said they had no trouble—no visitors or peeping Toms.

He looked tired, and his cheek was swollen. He hadn't taken the prescription pain meds this morning, because they kept him knocked out and he needed his faculties. Didn't appear the over-the-counter pills were doing the job. Neither of them had days to rest and recuperate, though. The killer wasn't going to give them a grace period. Now they were weak and vulnerable. If

Brigitte was the killer, she'd make a move sooner rather than later, while she had the upper hand.

"Debbie Deardon attended a free art history class at the museum in Los Artes. You have any idea who might have taught it?" His face reddened. "Actually, you wouldn't. You'd only have been thirteen. Wow. Um... okay, never mind." He cleared his throat and massaged the back of his neck.

"If it was at the art gallery, I know the owner, Mina. She and her husband, Raphe, have owned it for more than twenty years, and occasionally they hold classes."

It was nearing dinnertime. The day had been full of digging but no leads. She'd need to check on Dad soon.

"Why don't we wrap up here, check on your father then swing by the art gallery and talk to the owners?" He stacked a few case files.

"That sounds great. There's a little pizza joint down the street from Sunny Days. We could get a pie before going home. I've been eating pizza there since I was even younger than thirteen." Yeah, she'd added some bite. Just because she was a young teenager when these victims were murdered didn't mean she couldn't do her job to help them now. But clearly her age bugged Duke. "And I mean back to my house. Not home. I didn't imply my house was your house—though I do hope you feel welcome, as if it is your home. But it's not. So..." *Open mouth. Insert foot. What a heel. Oh, the puns.* She badly needed some help here.

Duke chuckled. "I know what you meant. And I do feel comfortable and welcome in your home. And for the record, I have no problem with how young you are affecting the *case*. You do good work, Brigitte."

The emphasis on the word *case* had her wondering.

Did he have a problem with her age personally? That seemed unfair, not that she was going to strike up a personal relationship, though the idea had some zing to it. Either way. "Thank you. And I have no problem with how old you are affecting the case. If you're wondering."

Duke smirked and arched an eyebrow. "I wasn't."

They collected their things, and Duke followed her to her car, since his rental was blown up and all. She ran inside Sunny Days and checked on Dad while Duke waited in the lobby. Her father was dozing, so she peeked in on Mrs. Kipling, who was in a recliner by the window.

"Mrs. Kipling? It's me, Brigitte."

The older woman's mouth turned up, squishing the wrinkles around her milky eyes. Her hair was in a braided bun at the nape of her neck, stark white and beautiful. She wore her usual tracksuit, but this one was pale pink to match her slippers. "Child, how are you? Vance said you'd been by the other night but I was sleeping."

"I was." She sat across from her in a desk chair and took her hands. "How are you feeling?"

"Oh, fine. Just fine," she said, as if she were bathed in sweet peace and joy. Her braille Bible rested in her lap. "Just been visiting with the Good Lord awhile. Nothing ever feels so bad after spending time in His word and in prayer. Heard some talk floating around the nurses' station about you."

"About me?" Brigitte hoped the news about her attacks hadn't reached Mrs. Kipling's ears. The local news had covered it, and in a small town, gossip spread like butter, quick and smooth-like, not to mention one had

happened on this property, but surely, they wouldn't tell that to Mrs. Kipling.

"Heard you been coming in with a Mr. Tall, Dark and Handsome. Is it true? You seeing someone?"

Brigitte wished she could become invisible. "Well, it's true, but not in the romantic sense. I mean, he is tall, and he's got rich, sepia-brown hair and sun-kissed skin and eyes like midnight without stars. A little silver starlight around his temples. Rugged, not polished. Kind, even though his voice is deep and gruff."

Mrs. Kipling's eyebrows twitched north. "I see. No, that's not romantic-sounding at all." She snickered and squeezed Brigitte's hands. "I've had my fill of what was romance and what was not. When I married Edward, he was spontaneous and whimsical. Oh, how I loved him. But he wasn't quite cut out to be a husband and had a selfish streak, and then he began drinking and that selfish streak coupled with abuse. He left when Vance was only twelve. But then I met Charlie, and he was the polar opposite. Practical. Dependable. Not at all polished or charming in the way Edward had been. But he was a rock and became a father to Vance in many ways his own father hadn't. I miss him so."

Mr. Kipling had died of cancer only ten years ago. Mrs. Kipling had talked of him often, but Brigitte had no idea she'd been married before him. "Heartaches come with life, don't they?"

"Oh, so many. But God has always been faithful. Through it all, I know He's never left me or disappointed me. Life can be disappointing. People most definitely. Hardships come with breathing. Just keep trusting Him, Brigitte. He's trustworthy."

"I know," she whispered. Just seemed life was too

hard at times, and when there was no break, no rest between new challenges and hardships, it was all too easy to wonder where God was or if He even cared. She was thankful for the encouragement from someone who had walked through their own share of grief and trouble but still could speak of God's goodness and love.

"It's a choice. Choose right."

She nodded and swallowed the lump in her throat.

"And I'd like to meet this rugged man who's been hanging around. I may not be able to see, but there's a lot a blind woman can recognize without her eyes." She grinned and patted Brigitte's hand.

"Well, I'll be sure to bring him by. I'm going to check on Dad one more time, then I've got a few things to do. Do you need anything?"

"No, child. I'm fine. Gonna read some and turn in early tonight. Don't go to sleep without reading the Good Book for yourself. You'll find answers you need in there. And most certainly some peace and rest."

"I will."

Mrs. Kipling's discipline to read her Bible was inspiring. Brigitte let days slip by without opening hers. Those were days of solace and truth she'd also let fade away. Tonight, she wasn't letting it go by. She kissed Mrs. Kipling's cheek and peeked in on Dad, who was now awake and fumbling through a nightstand drawer.

"Hi, Dad."

He looked up, startled. "I can't find the picnic basket."

Her heart sank. He wasn't lucid tonight. "What picnic basket?"

"Now, you know I take Mary to Big Bend National Park each year to celebrate the anniversary of our proposal. It has to be perfect. The cabin. The picnic. All of it."

How Dad could know the date of his proposal but forget Brigitte's name floored her, but he was right. This Saturday would be the day he proposed to Mom twenty-nine years ago. She didn't have the heart to tell him he wouldn't be going. But maybe for once she could go. They'd always gotten her a babysitter for the weekend. Dad's parents had been in Wisconsin and too far, and Mom's parents had both passed away before Brigitte's sixth birthday.

"Would you like to go Saturday?"

"Of course I would. If I can find the picnic basket." His brows knit, and his mouth straightened into a grim line.

"I have it." It was in the attic, and maybe going to the mountains would help him. Refocus him. Maybe it would unlock his mind, if only for a short time.

Relief flooded his face, and his shoulders relaxed. "Oh good. Good." He nodded and shuffled over to his recliner. "Is Mary here?"

"No, Dad. She's not here right now."

"Oh, well. I'm sure she'll be along shortly." He eased into his chair and reached for the TV remote. "She likes *Jeopardy*. Do you watch *Jeopardy*?"

"No. Not much."

"Well, I'll cook some dinner later, and we can watch it with her." Dad had always been the cook in the family. She frowned. Mom had never watched *Jeopardy* or any other show with them. Some of Dad's memories seemed made up.

"Sounds good. I'll be back later, okay?"

"Yes, yes. I'll see you later. What was your name again?"

Brigitte's eyes burned. "Brigitte."

"Oh, what a lovely name. I always thought so. I had a daughter named Brigitte."

Brigitte kissed his cheek. "I know. She loves you very much, too."

He grinned and flipped channels. She backed out of the room and wiped her eyes once she was out of sight. This was too much. Too hard.

Duke stood as she entered the lobby, and his smile sobered. "Is everything okay?"

Nothing was okay. The man she'd admired, looked up to and adored didn't even recognize her. A vicious killer was bent on destroying her, and she needed Dad more than ever. Needed his strong arms around her, reassuring her that she was safe. She'd always felt secure in his arms, but now…now they were frail and he didn't even know she was alive.

"No," she murmured honestly. No point in faking she was fine, and with Duke, she didn't feel like she had to.

His arms came around her, strong and steady, and she rested her head against his chest, hearing his solid heartbeat. "I'm sorry."

No platitudes. No ways to fix her problem—there wasn't one, anyway. No pep talks or advice. Just empathy and a place to rest her head. Exactly what she needed. Wanted. His right hand rested against the back of her head while his left firmly planted on her upper back.

She stood there, letting his comfort do its work. Who cared what gossip would erupt? In this moment, life stood still. Nothing bad could touch her. There was no darkness, only peace and light and safety.

Duke didn't rush her. Didn't loosen his grip. He stood steady, allowing her to take what she needed as long as she needed it.

No pressure. No romantic undertones. No hints of this possibly turning into something more, like a kiss.

Tears filled her eyes, and she squeezed them shut and hung on tighter, so grateful for this moment. For this man she barely knew but felt as if he had always known her.

Finally, she broke away and peered into his eyes. "Thank you. That's what I needed."

He brushed back a hair that had stuck to her wet cheek. "You're gonna be okay."

She needed to hear that, too, because it didn't feel like she was going to survive any of it. If the killer didn't get her, the loss of her mom and the slow decay of her father would. She slowly nodded, and Duke released his grip. "You hungry?" he asked.

"I could eat." She had little appetite, but it had been hours since she'd had a bite of food and she needed the fuel.

"Let's order that pizza and then visit the art gallery."

She nodded and followed him to the parking lot. "You ever been to Big Bend National Park?"

He chuckled. "I never know what's going to come out of your mouth, Brig. I like that. You're always a fun surprise. And no, I haven't."

Well, that didn't help her in the feels department. Unfortunately, the only surprises she'd been experiencing lately were fatal. She tried not to think about the danger she was in, but as they walked across the street to Italia, she couldn't help but feel as though murderous eyes were upon her.

Los Artes Gallery was in the heart of the small downtown district. Large floor-to-ceiling windows and

a colorful ranch-style porch. Inside, the white walls were hung with bright paintings, mostly landscapes, but a few varieties of abstract art and a couple of portraits.

Duke was way out of his element in here. What he had hanging on his walls at home was what Deena had picked out and not taken in the divorce. As far as style, he didn't have one. Simple suits in black, gray and navy. Basic jeans and T-shirts. He had a great pair of cowboy boots, but he rarely wore them. If he lived in Texas, he definitely would. Probably own three or four pair.

A woman who reminded him of a foxtail, slender with bushy, wheaten hair, approached. "Brigitte! So good to see you." Slight northern accent, definitely not native. Her smile was genuine, but her crystal-blue eyes inspected Duke with caution. "What can I do for you today? I haven't sold your latest piece yet, but I do have a check for you for the desert morning you did. Quite a nice one."

"Oh—" her cheeks reddened "—that's great. I don't think this latest piece is going to sell. But I appreciate you trying. I actually came to discuss a case. One involving the murder of Debbie Deardon. Would you remember her? It's been almost two decades." She pointed to Duke and introduced him.

The woman shook his hand and rested her other one on her throat. Uncomfortable with the situation. Who wouldn't be? "The name sounds familiar, but I can't place a face or why. I usually remember the artists that have pieces in the gallery."

"Debbie wouldn't have had an art piece hanging. She was the second victim of the Sunrise Serial Killer fifteen years ago. Family told us she took a free art his-

tory class here in Los Artes, where she lived. I know you and Raphe—"

A deep, bellowing voice sounded from the back. "Mina. I got those canvases you asked for." Shoes clicked on hardwood, and a sophisticated man with salt-and-pepper hair approached, a confused but congenial grin on his face. Dark eyes met Duke's. "Hello. I'm sorry. I didn't know we have company. I'm Raphe LaMont."

Duke shook his hand. "Special Agent Duke Jericho."

The smile faltered as he glanced at his wife. "How can we be of help, Agent?" He turned to Brigitte. "So good of you to come by. I have a check for you."

"We're here about Debbie Deardon."

"One of the Sunrise's victims?"

"You keep up with the story?" Duke asked.

"Well, it's hard not to. Debbie, another victim and the newest one were residents here in Los Artes." He swallowed hard, and his Adam's apple bobbed.

"Did Debbie ever attend an art history class that either of you might have given? Brigitte says you've done several free classes over the years."

"Quite right," he said. "We live to bring art culture to surrounding communities. I do believe she did attend one before she died. It's been so long, though."

"Can you get us a list of attendees for that one? Tell us anything you might remember about her? Did she have friends in the class—a male friend, maybe?" Duke asked.

"Wow, I can't say. The only reason I remember her at all is because of her unfortunate death. But I can pull up a class roster for you." He scuffled to the back office, and Mina sighed.

"I remember Debbie now. She had such enthusiasm about art history. She made pottery and sold it at flea markets and festivals. Very talented. Even had a few pieces in the Bluebell Boutique in Gran Valle."

So she was an artist, just not necessarily a painter. "That's useful information. Thank you."

Mr. LaMont returned with a roster in hand. Duke thanked him for it. Raphe also handed Brigitte a check for her piece.

She grinned. "It's crazy someone buys something I created. I'll never get over that."

"Where's the newest painting you're not so sure will sell?" Duke asked. He'd like to see it for himself. She had a few pieces in her home, but not many.

"It's in the back. I recently decided to try and sell it, but only because I need the money. It's not my best work—a little darker than normal, but it fit my mood at the time I painted it. I'd just put Dad in Sunny Days." She pointed toward the back wall.

Duke meandered over. Brigitte remained. Guess she didn't want to see him critique it. Hanging on the far right was a sixteen by twenty of a desert night. A full moon. A silver coyote howling and stars that appeared to twinkle right off the canvas. The piece was labeled *Desert Moonlight*.

It was breathtaking. Not the soft pastels he'd seen in her house, but dark blues, blacks and yellows. Even a hint of purple. It was dark, but even on this backdrop, light shined, like glimmers of hope that within the night there was beauty to be seen and that dawn would break eventually.

Duke felt her presence beside him. He slowly turned and caught her questions, anxiety in her eyes.

"Not quite the upbeat piece I typically paint. Like I said, it was a dark time, and I suppose the grief and loss spilled onto the canvas."

She was making excuses. Vulnerable. Unsure. "I think it's great. I don't see only darkness and grief."

"No? What do you see?" She scraped her top teeth along her bottom lip, rubbed her palms against her thighs and shifted her weight back and forth, awaiting his view of her work.

"Hope. Light at the end of the tunnel. A new day about to dawn. You don't?" He studied her face, noting the way her eyes dilated and her jaw unclenched. Her fists relaxed, and the tension in her shoulders released as she observed her painting.

"No," she whispered. "I mean… I see what you're seeing now that you bring it to my attention, but when I painted it—I never saw anything positive or hope to look forward to."

Duke inhaled deeply. When he'd been at his worst moments, he hadn't seen any light or hope, either. "I suppose when we're in the thick of things, our perception is skewed, dimmed. But deep within you, the light spilled its way onto the canvas. I suppose your faith was there all along, though you didn't see it, but that's what faith is. Not seeing but believing, even when it doesn't feel like there's a shining moment."

Her gaze met his and she smiled, but it was her eyes that sent his heart into a steady gallop and his stomach into a twister. He had to fight off the tug. When he was twenty-five she was only thirteen, and that was creepy.

"Your job requires deep thinking, so I'm not sure why I'm surprised at your wise insight and poetic view. I like it."

Those same three words he'd used about how much she surprised him. He liked that she liked it. Too much. "Or maybe I've just been around a lot longer than you."

"You have a thing about age. How old are you?"

"Almost forty."

"I know people far older than you, Duke Jericho, and they don't have a single brain cell in their head. Barely can articulate a complete sentence. It's not your age that makes you wise. It's your faith applied to life circumstances, and you can have a lot of life tossed at you at any age."

Proof was in her own wise words. Maybe he was simply testing her to see what she thought about their age difference. It mattered to him. Did it matter to her?

He observed her again, the way her eyes shone and remained dilated. Didn't seem to matter. But even if he could get past the twelve years, he'd made a mess of a marriage once, and it wouldn't be fair to himself or Brigitte if he acted on his strong feelings and it went somewhere good, only to nose-dive into the toilet later.

"I stand corrected, Miss Linsey." His phone rang, and he answered the unknown number. "Agent Jericho."

"Hello, uh, this is Hannah Harker. My sister was Jamie Harker. My mom said you were looking into her case and had a few questions." He covered the phone and whispered who was on the other end for Brigitte.

"Yes, we do. Could you hold on for a moment?" He waited for her to agree, then muted the phone. "Thank you for your time," he said to Raphe and Mina. "If we need anything further, we'll let you know."

They exited the gallery, and once inside Brigitte's Jeep, he put the phone on speaker. "Okay, Miss Harker. We'd love to talk to you."

"Mom said you asked if Jamie was an artist. She's not. But... I am. I work with communities who are trying to salvage older parts of town that have been vandalized or tagged."

"Tagged?"

"Graffiti artists or gangs who cover buildings to mark territory. I repaint the walls to brighten it up. I'm actually working in a small business district on the edge of Gran Valle now."

*Interesting.* "Do you know if Jamie had been stalked or followed within the weeks maybe even months prior to her death?"

Silence filled the line before Hannah answered.

"I didn't think it was anything at the time, but over the years, I've had time to ruminate. She mentioned a few times that someone had to have stolen some stuff from her, or else she was losing her mind. We laughed it off, but one night we did see a man sitting across the street from her house. I hollered at him and he drove off."

"Did you see his face?"

"Sort of. It was dark. But it's been a long time."

"Could we come by now? I have a forensic sketch artist with me."

"Jamie, I'm Brigitte Linsey, the forensic artist. I might be able to help you remember, even if it's been a long time. I'd like to at least try."

"Of course." She gave them the address to the warehouse. Brigitte noted she was familiar with the area. They hung up and headed the twenty minutes to Gran Valle.

The run-down older district had been rebuilt farther north about ten years ago, according to Brigitte's chatter

on the way there. Now these buildings, many vacant, had been riddled with vagrants and what appeared to be teenage and gang graffiti.

"Every town, even small towns, have a dark side, a run-down side—a forgotten side." Brigitte parked catty-corner from the old brick warehouse Hannah Harker was painting; it was sandwiched between two smaller, vacant brick buildings. "It's awful to be forgotten."

Duke glanced at her as she stared at the old, empty, neglected building. She wasn't looking for answers—simply making a statement—so Duke refrained from speaking. Sometimes silence spoke better than words. Instead, he lightly touched her shoulder to let her know he heard her. Felt for her. Then he waited for her to exit, and he followed suit.

The sun had set as they drove to Gran Valle. Clouds rolled on the night sky, revealing rain in the future again. Just as the thought crossed his mind, a big, fat drop splattered on his forehead. It was cool and a re-prieve from the heat, which was taking no prisoners.

"We should hurry before the bottom drops out." Duke picked up his pace, and Brigitte mimicked him. As they raced into the warehouse, a boom splintered the air.

Not thunder.

A bullet slammed into the brick next to Brigitte, and she shrieked, then hit the pavement.

"Brig!"

# EIGHT

Brigitte had dropped to the ground when she felt the sting along her bicep, the burning sensation ripping through her, and then the sky opened up and buckets poured down, drenching her in seconds.

"Brig!" Duke called again, and his hand was on her arm, her cheeks. "You've been hit!"

Another bullet hit the ground beside them, and Duke snatched her up and sprinted into the warehouse.

"I'm okay. I'm…" Shocked. Stunned. "I can stand."

A window shattered nearby—the shooter taking random aim with hopes he might hit someone.

"Hello," a voice called.

"Get down!" Duke bellowed. "Active shooter!"

Hannah Harker screeched, and items clattered to the ground.

"Are you hurt?" Duke called.

"No. I thought it was thunder until I heard the window shatter. I'm about twenty feet west of you, behind the brick wall."

"Stay put. Stay down." He cupped Brigitte's cheek. "I need to see the wound. You're bleeding."

"I don't think it's too bad. A graze or a through and

through. The bullet hit the brick." But the third time might be the charm.

Brigitte was wearing an elbow-length shirt. She scooched the sleeve up, but it wasn't far enough. She slipped her arm into her shirt and brought it out through the scoop neck with a wince.

Duke peeped out the window. Thunder belched, and the rain pummeled the warehouse roof. They couldn't be sure if the sniper was still out there or not. "I don't see anything, but it's raining so hard, it's impossible anyway." He glanced down at her bare arm, streaked with blood, and inspected the wound. "You might need a butterfly stitch, but the Lord and the rain were your saving grace. Whoever is firing isn't a professional. A pro wouldn't have missed, not even in a thunderstorm."

Brigitte's stomach twisted, and her heart rate moved at dangerous speeds. Duke grabbed his cell phone and called Gran Valle police for backup.

"Let's wait it out in safety. Once he sees police lights, he surely won't be so foolish to stick around."

"Hannah," Duke hollered. "How you doing?"

"Okay." Her voice was shaky and shallow.

"I'm good to move. Really." Brigitte shifted. "We need to get to Hannah." A deafening clang, like a huge pipe falling on concrete, had Duke and Brigitte drawing their weapons, and Brigitte's breath caught.

"Came from Hannah's direction," Brigitte whispered, and Duke nodded then motioned for Brigitte to back him up. Her upper arm throbbed and burned, but she focused on the task ahead. Keeping close to the walls and brick pillars for cover, Brigitte inched behind Duke as they set off toward the noise.

If it had been caused by Hannah, she'd have called out. Someone was inside.

Adrenaline raced through Brigitte's body, but she kept a solid grip on her gun, her hand steady and her eyes alert. Duke's life depended on it.

Duke crouched behind a floor-to-ceiling brick pillar and looked back at Brigitte. He motioned he was about to dart the six feet to the next pillar, and she'd back him up as she ran for the one he was standing behind now for her own cover.

Rain pelted the roof, keeping them from hearing any quiet movement. Thunder rumbled as if it was in the building itself, and then Hannah shrieked as gunfire cracked.

Duke fired back, knowing where Hannah was crouched and making sure not to aim in her direction. A figure darted behind a column, then raced toward the south side of the warehouse. Duke pursued. "Check on Hannah!"

Brigitte frowned. Duke shouldn't be chasing after the shooter alone, and not in this kind of dark and threatening downpour.

Hannah cried out, "Help!" No more time to be irritated over Duke's renegade move. She found Hannah hunched behind an old, deteriorating cardboard box and clutching her shoulder, which was soaked with blood.

Sirens wailed. It felt like hours, but it had only been a few fleeting moments since Duke had called them. "Help is on the way. I'm Brigitte. Can I see the wound?"

Hannah nodded, her face twisted in pain. It was a lot of blood. A little lower and it would have been right in the chest. Why would the killer want to kill Hannah? Had he mistaken her for Brigitte? If that was the

case, she might never forgive herself. Brigitte slowly inspected the wound then applied pressure.

Lightning illuminated the building, and Brigitte got a good look at Hannah's face. Pale and drooping eyes. "Hey, stay awake. You're going to be fine, but you need to stay awake. Can you hear me?"

"Yes," she said. "Was that the man I saw all those years ago?"

"I don't know." He must have followed Duke and Brigitte without them spotting him, and they'd led him straight to Jamie Harker's sister.

But she hadn't died. She would live.

Paramedics arrived, and two of them loaded Hannah on a stretcher while another butterflied Brigitte. Now to find Duke. She darted in the direction he'd run, past the main warehouse floor.

The door to the west entrance was open, rain pouring in sheets. Brigitte ran into the night but kept close to the brick walls. Where was he? She sprinted down the alley sandwiched between the buildings, her feet squishy from running through standing water and puddles. The rain plastered her hair to her head, and her clothing was drenched and heavy against her. She swung a right and jogged along the back of the next building, water running in her eyes and making it difficult to see.

Up ahead she made out a figure. "Freeze!"

"It's me! It's Duke." She lowered her weapon and he ran toward her. "I lost him. I'm sorry."

"If you're going to be sorry, be sorry for taking off like some lone wolf and scaring me half to death. That was unprofessional, reckless and flat out stupid!"

Chest heaving and his own hair a wet cap on his

head, he smirked. "Well, Officer Linsey, tell me how you really feel."

Her blood raced hot. "Really? You're going to make jokes. What if you had been shot? It's nuts out here," she hollered over the storm. "You could have died! I can't have that on my conscience. I already nearly got a man killed. Hannah's been shot. I can't say if she'll truly be okay, but I think so. I deserve an apology—and a partner with some common sense!"

His smirk faded and his eyes fixed on hers; nothing about his facial expression was comical. "I am sorry, Brigitte. You're right. I shouldn't have been so reckless. I was thinking…"

Duke's warm hand melded against her cheek, and she searched his eyes.

"Thinking?"

He expelled a heavy breath. "I was thinking about you." He held her gaze as rain ran down his matted hair in rivulets, streaking his stubbly cheeks.

"Well, I was thinking about you," she whispered. How terrified she'd been seeing him jet off without any help and knowing a desperate and vicious killer was out there alone with him. That terror—if she was being honest—went past professional concern. A world without Duke Jericho in it was a world with too many gray undertones. With no soft yellows against a backdrop of darkness.

"I know," he said as his eyes remained locked on hers and his head began an achingly slow dip toward her lips.

"I don't think you do." Or maybe he did. She'd never been one to hide her feelings, even if she had reservations about him—about herself. Her heart couldn't care

less and was about to burst from her chest as his lips grazed against hers.

"Officer Linsey! Agent Jericho!" a deep voice boomed, and Duke pulled away, his eyes once sharp and clear with intent now cloudy with confusion.

Clearing his throat, he waved. "Over here. We lost the suspect." He shot Brigitte a pained look and jogged away toward the Gran Valle detective calling their names. Disappointment lodged in her throat, and rejection formed a lump in her gut. That last expression before he left her...the look of regret mixed with his confusion. Right now he was likely asking himself why in the world he'd nearly kissed an artsy twentysomething in the middle of West Texas.

She was asking why she was about to kiss a man when she knew it could go nowhere. On a billion levels. This wasn't like her at all.

But even with all the reasons, no one had ever made her feel so far above average. He saw her as smart, savvy and brave. He valued her opinion and listened to her express her thoughts about art. He observed her worst painting and could easily spot the beauty that she hadn't even recognized. When she was with Duke Jericho, she felt completely safe, respected and not so much needed but wanted.

She felt seen. Known.

Hannah Harker had been injured with a through-and-through bullet, then stitched up and given pain meds. She was staying overnight for observation. She slumped in her hospital bed, and Brigitte knew she didn't have much time before Hannah crashed from the meds.

"Hannah, we are so sorry about what happened." Bri-

gitte laid a gentle hand on her arm, and Duke stood at the foot of the bed. After they gave their statements to Detective Collins, they'd driven straight to Gran Valle General and waited on news about Hannah and her condition. Guilt nipped at Brigitte for standing over a woman who'd been shot, only to ask her for information. Seemed insensitive. But Hannah might now be a target if the killer knew she had useful information. Gran Valle had placed an officer at the door for that very purpose. But no point in terrifying the woman further.

"You said you sort of saw the man who'd been in his car outside Jamie's home. You hollered at him, and he drove away. And that she mentioned things had gone missing from her house. Can you remember what those items might have been?"

Now was not the time to whip out her sketch pad. Hannah's faculties weren't sharp. Brigitte glanced at Duke, and he leaned over the bed. "Hannah, can you recall the items she thought were missing?"

"I can't remember. I'm sorry."

Could be the meds fogging her recall. "Did you tell the police about this? Make a report?"

"Not official. But we told a friend of the family who works for Gran Valle PD."

Duke flashed Brigitte a hopeful expression. "Name?"

"Chris. Chris Collins. He's a detective."

Detective Collins had taken their report and never once mentioned he knew Hannah, and he hadn't mentioned on the homicide report he'd been notified of stalking. Could be because he felt bad for not taking it seriously—if that were the case—or it could be negligence.

Or something else.

\* \* \*

Duke sipped his coffee as he stood inside the Gran Valle PD conference room. After talking to Hannah Harker at Gran Valle General, Brigitte had driven them back to her place—mostly in silence—so they could get dry and get some rest. After the shoot-out it had been chaos, and by the time they'd arrived at her house, it had been almost eleven o'clock.

Brigitte had given a simple good-night after asking if there was anything he needed. His answer had been no, but he needed a time machine to go back several hours, before he'd attempted to kiss her. What had he been thinking?

He'd been thinking about her. It had been reckless to run off after a dangerous killer without backup. But his only thought was to subdue the suspect and make Brigitte safe. Protecting her had been the motivation behind sprinting after the Sunrise Serial Killer.

And he'd scared her half to death in the process. If something had happened to him, she would have lived with the guilt—unwarranted, but guilt nonetheless. That wasn't fair to her. Then she'd stood vulnerable and honest in the pouring rain, and once again he'd been led by emotion and not the good sense God gave him.

He regretted the near kiss, and he regretted not being able to finish what he'd started. That tiny taste wasn't enough, and it had kept him frustrated on so many levels last night as he warred with the motives behind wanting to kiss her and talking himself out of never doing it again.

Besides, as soon as the killer was caught, he was returning to Virginia and fieldwork and his empty house and mostly frozen dinners he ate on the couch while

watching the Discovery or Travel channel. Then he'd slog to a big bed alone. No partner to share his life with.

Not much of a life. More like existence. But the thought of another relationship slipping through his buttery fingers was too much. The idea of being betrayed again—not that Brigitte would, but then, he'd never expected Deena to be unfaithful, either. There was no guarantee on a full life with someone. He'd misled Brigitte. Misled himself.

He'd have to talk to her at some point. The tension wasn't terrible, but it was there, like a thin veil between them. At the moment, she'd run next door to the diner to grab some breakfast burritos. Duke tossed his empty foam cup in the trash and left the interview room. Detective Chris Collins had been on the force for over thirty years and investigated Tina Wheeler, Debbie Deardon, Adley Portman and presently Kayla Lowe's cases. He hadn't investigated Jamie Harker's because she was found in the desert near Los Artes, and their police handled her case. But he hadn't passed on the stalking information Hannah had gone to him about, nor had he ever filed an official complaint report from Jamie or Hannah. Why?

He walked into the bullpen, scanning the desks for the detective. He was sitting in a small cubicle near the corner. "Detective," Duke said, observing his body language. His wide smile screamed friendly, but his dark eyes were cautious.

"How can I help you, Agent?"

"Some new light's been shed concerning Jamie Harker's case." He relayed the newest information about Hannah and what she'd shared before her pain meds kicked in.

"There you are," Brigitte said as she entered the bull-pen with a white paper sack. The smells of bacon and sausage wafted in his direction, and his stomach rumbled. "I've got food."

She nodded at Detective Collins, and he returned it.

"I was just updating Detective Collins. Is there any particular reason, Detective, you didn't report that someone might have been taking things from Jamie's house and that Hannah caught a guy in the car and hollered at him, waving him off? Or why you didn't mention knowing the victim and her family personally? That seems pertinent to me."

Collins's face scrunched, and his neck flushed red. "My personal relationship is irrelevant, and Jamie Harker had bipolar disorder. When she was in a state of mania, she would sometimes have paranoia. When she told me that she thought things were being taken from her home or misplaced, I talked to her mother about her meds. She'd been off them. I had no reason at that time to think anything was actually happening—and to be honest, I still don't, so that's why I never formally filed a report."

So far it made sense.

"When Hannah said someone had been across the street and she yelled at him, I knew she took Jamie seriously about the missing items. She lived in denial that her sister had a mental illness. For all I knew, a guy was eating a hot dog waiting on a friend, and Hannah freaked him out. It's pretty cut-and-dried."

Nothing was ever cut-and-dried when it came to homicide.

"Look, there were no reports of family or friends stating previous victims had been stalked," Detective

Collins said. "Except Jamie Harker, and then Adley Portman, but by the time we got wind of that, Jamie was already gone, and due to her typical behavior off meds, I still can't say solidly I believe her accusations."

"What about her phone records? She had a same number call her once a week for four weeks leading up to her death. You didn't go over phone records?"

"Why would I? There was no reason to believe he was calling victims, and we had no basis, no pattern of calls."

"We found a pattern, Detective. Burner phones, but the same time frame. Once a week. Four weeks leading up to murders."

"Well, I guess that's why they pay you the big bucks. To be infallible." He stood, his hands balled in fists and jaw clenched. "Don't come in here telling me how to do my job or critiquing my methods. I worked with what I had, just like I'm doing with Kayla Lowe. We didn't catch the card between the stove and counter. True. But even you almost missed it. We are not being neglectful or lazy."

Duke's pulse spiked as the detective inched into his face, though Collins was a couple inches shorter.

"Then you know that we found the same phone pattern with Kayla, and she told the owner and manager of the florist shop she felt stalked and that someone had been in her place, too."

Collins's narrowed eyes said he had no idea. "I haven't talked to the florist yet, and it doesn't help Jamie Harker now, anyway."

It'd been days. Where had he been? What was he doing? Appeared to be nothing, but he had made it clear

he wasn't being lazy or neglectful. Seemed like he was being exactly that.

"We saved you a trip, then. Have you even been inside Kayla's home?"

"Of course I have." His nostrils flared.

"And what did you have to say about those flowers?"

"Without the initial card it meant nothing nefarious! Still may not."

Brigitte cleared her throat. "I think we should eat before it gets cold. We have a lot of ground to cover today."

Duke glanced at her and read her expression—he should back down. She was right. Getting angry and angering a detective he was supposed to be working in tandem with wasn't exactly good politics. But Duke was never one to play team sports.

"Fine," he said and followed her into the interview room.

"You'll catch more flies with honey. Just sayin'."

"I know." He took his burrito from her hand and unwrapped the top half, then bit into it. Southwestern, with a kick of jalapeño at the end. "I just think he's doing sloppy work."

"That may be true, but he won't be of any assistance if we need him." She plunked down on the hard metal chair and bit into her breakfast burrito, steam pluming in front of her face. "I want to visit Hannah again when she's more lucid and see if I can't get a decent sketch of the man she saw. I know it was dark, but with the other sketches we might be able to tell more about his features. What else can we do?"

"Good question." Duke's phone rang and he answered. "Agent Jericho."

"Agent, this is Patty from the Quantico lab."

He dropped his burrito on the table and put her on speaker.

"We got a partial off that pinkie ring from the first victim, Tina Wheeler."

Finally, a bread crumb. "Excellent. Who's it belong to?"

"A Faith Roswell. Forty-three years old. Lives in Los Artes."

"Thank you. Anything else?" He'd given them all the old evidence so they could use new technology and run prints and DNA again. Someone who wasn't in the system back then might be now.

"No—still working on it, though."

"Good work." He hung up and smiled. "We have a trail to go down. I'll get the address for Faith Roswell, and we'll see if she has any connection to Tina Wheeler."

Brigitte was nearly done with her burrito. "Good plan."

He paused at the door. They hadn't even mentioned that near kiss. Should he? No. Now wasn't the time.

After retrieving Faith Roswell's address, they drove the twenty miles south. Off a small highway in the middle of the desert was a mobile home surrounded by a rock garden filled with cacti.

"She's quite the loner, out here on the outskirts of Los Artes. Not another house within miles."

"Maybe she's a recluse." Duke clambered out of the passenger side of Brigitte's Jeep as they walked up to the dusty trailer house. Duke rapped on the flimsy metal door. Inside, a vacuum cleaner whirred, and noise from the TV sounded over it. He rapped harder.

The vacuum halted, and the TV volume lowered. A

woman with short red hair and tired eyes appeared. She glanced from Duke to Brigitte. "Help ya?"

Duke showed his creds and Brigitte her badge. "We'd like to ask you a few questions regarding a Tina Wheeler." He held up her picture. "Do you know her?"

Her lips pursed as she studied the picture, lines around her mouth tightening like most women who smoked more than a few packs a day. "No. I don't recognize her. Should I?"

"Do you recognize this?" Duke held up a photo of the silver pinkie ring with a heart in the center.

Faith's eyes widened, and her hand went to her throat. "I—uh… I don't think so. You need to leave now."

"Wait!" Brigitte called. "Please. Let us come in. You could help us, and I believe you know you can."

They waited a beat, and the glass door separating them creaked open.

"Do you recognize this ring?" Duke asked.

Faith nodded. "It's mine."

The fact she was surprised to see a picture of it and then wanted them to go twisted in his gut. Whatever Faith might reveal wasn't going to be pleasant to discuss.

They entered her modest abode. Clean with a faint hint of lemon and stale cigarette smoke. She offered them seats on the plain brown sofa, then she perched on the recliner across from them, her hands balled on her lap.

"Miss Roswell, can you tell us how your ring may have ended up on Tina Wheeler?"

She shook her head. "I don't know Tina Wheeler. I have no idea how she got my ring. I mean, it may not even be mine. It could be one like it."

"But you did have a ring like this and now you don't?" Duke asked, using as much tenderness as possible. Faith Roswell was vulnerable, and that ring held no good memory, from what he gathered observing her body language. And he wondered if her living out here alone and secluded had anything to do with that ring.

Brigitte sat beside him quietly, bringing a gentleness to the atmosphere next to his imposing presence. He was thankful she was here.

Faith nodded. "It was stolen from me."

"When?"

"Twenty-three years ago."

That was precise. Too precise, which indicated it had been relevant or traumatic. "Can you tell me about that?"

She rubbed her palms along her thighs. "What happened to Tina Wheeler?"

Duke looked to Brigitte. A softer touch was needed. His gut screamed to be gentle. Brigitte met his eyes and then turned to Faith, recognizing his silent request. She was intuitive. He admired that.

"Tina Wheeler was the first victim of the Sunrise Serial Killer. Have you heard any of the news stories about him?"

Tears filled her eyes, and she nodded. "She might be his first deceased victim, but I don't think she's his first victim, not after you showing me the ring and telling me she had worn it." She hurriedly wiped her cheeks. Brigitte waited patiently for Faith to continue, and he also admired her keen sense of when to let a victim lead according to their own comfort.

"I was twenty. It was late, and I was getting off work at the Gran Valle Grocery. I didn't see him. He came

from behind in the dark. He hit me, and I blacked out. When I awoke, I was in the desert. In Gran Valle, I realized later." Tears leaked from her eyes as she told of her brutal attack in an empty, cold desert.

"I'm so sorry, Faith," Duke said and meant every word. No one should have to fear leaving work at night. This should never happen. "Did you ever see his face? The vehicle he transported you in?"

"I can't remember the vehicle, but I saw his face."

Hope soared. This was the break they needed. "Good. Did he say anything to you?"

"He said my eyes looked like a lovely star before sunrise." Those words broke her, and she collapsed in sobs. Brigitte went to her, embraced her and let her release that horrific night in tears. "I didn't go to the police. Didn't tell anyone. I was…ashamed."

"It wasn't your fault," Duke said. "You did nothing wrong. You survived. That's a brave thing."

She sniffed and expelled a shaky breath. "After, he took my ring. He called it a token."

He hadn't stolen it from a random place, but off the very finger of his victim. Tina Wheeler wore little gold hoops, but there had been no earrings in her ears. Jamie Harker had been found with little gold hoops, but her boyfriend had asked about the pearl earrings he gave her that she always wore.

Duke's gut clenched, and blood drained from his head, leaving him dizzy. This killer wasn't stealing random jewelry. He was lifting jewelry from victims and replacing it on new victims. Kayla Lowe always wore a necklace, but it was missing, and beside her had been a brooch. Could she have been wearing both items and he took them? Why both? It was possible he hadn't had

the chance to wipe prints from the brooch and Brigitte had interrupted him placing it on her and removing prints, so he'd swiped it.

And that meant he knew his prints were in the system.

The Sunrise Serial Killer assaulted and strangled his victims. Faith had been allowed to live. It was possible that she had been one of his early victims, possibly the first before he worked up the courage to begin murdering them.

"Faith, I'm sorry to make you have to remember, but after he attacked you, what happened?"

Faith grasped Brigitte's hand for support. "He put his hand around my neck, and I thought I was going to die. I passed out. When I awoke, it was morning and I was alone in the desert. He was gone." She told how she found the road, and a man in a semitruck stopped and helped her. He drove her to the grocery store. She got in her car and went home. Never spoke of it again until now.

"One more tough question. Can you describe him to Officer Linsey? She's also a forensic artist. His likeness on paper can help us find him, keep him from doing this to others."

She nodded, and Brigitte withdrew her sketch pad and pencil from her bag. "I should tell you that, well, he keeps up with me."

"What do you mean?" A ball of ice chilled his gut.

"Every year on the date it happened, I get a card in the mail. *Happy Anniversary.* No signature or writing. No postmark. He hand delivers it. I've moved so many times. Last year I moved here. Still, somehow he finds me."

"I'm sorry," Brigitte said.

This guy got sicker by the second. "That's good to know. Do you keep them—the cards?"

"No, I burn them."

So much for prints.

"Okay, Faith, let's get started. What do you remember most about him?" Brigitte asked.

"His smell." She shuddered. "Cologne. Normally I would have admired it. Now I can hardly stand to smell it."

How was she going to draw a smell?

"That's good. Now that you're back there, you come to, and what do you see?"

Faith closed her eyes. "His eyes."

"Good. Good. Describe them the best you can."

She spent the next ten minutes asking questions and working patiently with Faith, letting her pause and take the time necessary to keep going. Her kindness and empathy made its way into his heart, his very marrow. Tough, tenacious and tender all at once. He'd never met anyone like Brigitte Linsey. Not in all his life.

The composite was coming together. The eyes, dark and almond-shaped, with thick brows and a straight nose. Squared jaw. Not the kind of man a woman might shy away from. He'd appeared to be in his early twenties. Brigitte would have to do an age progression. But that now put him anywhere from late forties to late fifties, possibly.

"Okay, almost done. I'm so proud of you, Faith," Brigitte said.

Duke opened his mouth to finish their interview, just as the window in the living room shattered and a bullet splintered the wooden paneling. "On the floor!"

# NINE

Duke dived onto the floor as bullets sprayed the living room. Brigitte had tossed Faith to the floor, and Duke hovered over them while glass rained down. "We need to get out of this house." It was like being sardines in a can. "Back door. Go."

The living room opened into the kitchen and the back door, which was only a few feet away, but there was no cover from the stretch of desert to the mountains. Cacti weren't even close to providing cover. Going out the front was suicide.

Duke thought fast as they army crawled toward the kitchen, wincing at bits of glass that littered the carpet, but they had no choice. Bullets shattered the small kitchen window. "Do you have a vehicle out back?"

"No. But my brother keeps his side-by-side here. For desert riding."

"Seating?"

"Four."

They cowered near the back door. "It's only a matter of time before he realizes we're going out the back." Duke gripped his weapon and slowly stood to see out the glassless kitchen window. A large black four-wheel-

drive truck was on the side of the empty road, but he couldn't make out the driver. The truck would take desert terrain easily.

"How far back is the UTV?"

"Parked by the little shed, about ten feet," Faith said on a shaky breath.

Brigitte laid a hand on Faith's shoulder. "It's okay. We'll keep you safe."

Faith's eyes filled with tears. "Is it him? The man who hurt me?"

Duke's jaw clenched. The woman had been through enough and was out here living a quiet life. Their investigation had stirred the pot and the sludge was now rising to the top, invading what she'd tried to simmer away all these years.

"I can't say for sure. Right now, we need to worry about getting us all safe. Brigitte, you take the rear and I'll lead us out. Faith, are the keys in the side-by-side?"

"No, they're on a hook in the utility shed. The key to the shed is hanging by the back door on that red lanyard." She pointed upward to the wall by the back door. Duke snatched them.

"Change of plans. I'm going to get the keys from the utility shed. When I have them, y'all make a run for it—Brigitte, cover Faith. Then we'll make a play to the mountains."

"I don't like that idea," Brigitte insisted.

"It's not up for debate. I'm pulling rank." If he didn't, she'd throw herself in the line of fire, and he wasn't having two women's potential deaths on his conscience. Not to mention if he saw Brigitte fall to the ground... nope. Not thinking about that. "Stay put or cover me

from here. But under no circumstances do you come after me. Take care of Faith."

Without another word, he surveyed the backyard. Nothing but mostly desert terrain, indigenous scenery and, beyond the dust, mountains. Not exactly chock-full of areas where they could find cover, but the mountains were their only shot.

He bolted for the utility shed, hearing shots fired at the trailer toward the bedroom. Any minute he'd come around back, knowing he'd eaten up the front of the trailer—if he was a smart killer. And he was. He'd been getting away with murder and apparent assault for decades.

Duke made it to the tin shed with a sagging rusty roof. He needed both hands, so he slid his gun into his holster and the key into the old padlock that was blocking their freedom.

The sound of an engine revving came closer.

The shooter was making his way right for them. And the second he rounded the corner, Duke was an open target. As the padlock released, bullets hit the shed, and a big black truck came into view.

Brigitte returned fire from the deck, hitting the windshield and spiderwebbing it. "Run, Faith!" she hollered.

Duke swung open the shed door, using it as a shield as bullets hit too close to home. Duke scanned the shed as Brigitte covered him. He snagged the keys and crouched low, sprinting for the side-by-side. Faith was already in the back seat, ducked down, and Brigitte was making her way toward it. She got another shot at the hood, and the truck gunned it around the shed, using it as a shield.

Duke reached the UTV right as Brigitte jumped in

the passenger side. He turned the ignition, and the small car-like vehicle with no roof, doors or windows roared to life. Not exactly much protection, but he hoped it went fast enough to be a better escape than a shield.

The model was older and a manual shift; he threw it in gear, thankful his first truck was a stick shift, and lay on the gas. "Faith, stay down."

She shrieked, and Brigitte shifted in the seat, her gun trained on the black truck that followed them.

"Can you see him?"

"No, the windows are tinted, and I think he's wearing a mask," Brigitte said in a strained voice. "Get closer to the mountains. We can get up trails his truck can't."

Zigzagging to make them a harder target, he obeyed Brigitte and beelined it for the craggy, looming rock ahead. A bullet hit the back end of the side-by-side, and Faith screeched.

"Are you hit?" Brigitte hollered over the roar of both vehicles.

Faith didn't reply.

Duke's heart rate ticked into dangerous levels. "Faith!"

Brigitte reached into the back seat while Duke kept his eye on the mountain ahead. Maybe about one hundred feet left until they could get to a trail and duck for cover.

"Duke, she's been shot. I'm not getting a pulse." Brigitte's voice was strangled but solid.

"Can you call it in?"

"No signal out this far. We're too close to the mountains."

There was no way to pull over, to get Faith out of the vehicle and keep them all safe. Adrenaline surged

through Duke's veins as he weighed the limited options. Brigitte shoved her gun in her waistband and went to work on Faith Roswell as Duke gunned it for the mountains.

Fifty feet.

Twenty…ten.

Duke glanced toward Brigitte. Her hands were covered in blood. "How bad is it?"

"I—I…it's bad, Duke. It's real bad."

A bullet hit their tire, and Duke suddenly lost control of the wheel as the tire blew. Brigitte pitched backward in her seat. They were so close. If he could get the steering wheel under control…

Up ahead, a narrow, dusty trail beckoned them to come. To find refuge in the craggy mountains. As they approached, the wheel hit a large rock and the UTV began to tip sideways. They could not flip. Duke jerked the wheel to the right, hoping to gain some balance as they approached the slim opening that gave them access to the mountains and got them out of open terrain and harm's way, where they could get a better handle on Faith's condition and save her if it wasn't too late.

Brigitte grabbed the side of the UTV as Duke yelled, "Hold on!"

And then they were on the bumpy trail, stirring up dust that enshrouded them, blocking his view ahead. The dirt clogged his throat and he coughed, and then the UTV rammed into a large boulder near the side of the rocky mountain, throwing Brigitte out. He couldn't see her, but he heard her as she screamed, then went deathly silent.

Heart jumping into his throat, he called her name, then called it again.

The killer's truck might not make it into the narrow opening, but he could easily come in on foot.

The dust they'd unleashed began to clear as he assessed Faith Roswell, but there was no lifesaving to be done. She was gone. She'd taken one to the back, and the damage was too much. She stared up with lifeless gray eyes, and a deep grief swept through Duke's chest.

He'd failed.

This woman had been scarred and was willing to help, and he hadn't even been able to keep her alive long enough to see that she would get justice on earth. He squeezed his eyes closed and prayed that this was not in vain. That he and Brigitte would find this monster bent on destroying her.

If he couldn't protect Faith, how was he going to keep Brigitte safe?

Clambering from the UTV, he scanned the area. About three feet away, she lay in a crumpled heap, but she was alive. He raced toward her, his body aching from the impact. Not much cushion to absorb a direct hit with something like a mountain.

She lay on the ground, dust turning to dirt on her sweaty cheeks and neck.

"Are you hurt? How bad?"

Rubbing her shoulder where she'd already been hit twice before, she sat upright, then her eyes widened. "Faith!"

Duke laid a gentle hand on her shoulder and shook his head. "She was gone seconds after she was shot—bled out."

Brigitte's face crumpled, and she lay back down in the dirt and rock, covering her face. "It's not your fault," he said. "You did everything you could to protect her."

"Three people have been injured and one has died because of me. That makes it my fault."

He leaned over her, removing her hands from her face, his body acting as a sun visor. "Look at me." She obeyed. "It makes it his fault. We have to investigate. We now know more than we ever have. Faith didn't die in vain, Brig. Without her information, we'd still think that the killer was ripping off homes or random people for jewelry or that it belonged to someone he knew. We now know he's taking items from victims and putting them on newer vics."

Brigitte nodded, but her eyes still held skepticism. He hauled her up and embraced her. "We're going to get him. I'm going to rework the profile with this new information, and we're going to go back through calls and reports of assault with the same MO as Faith, and something is going to pop. Because she might be an early victim, but not the first."

There might be others who never reported it, like Faith, but there could be at least one who did, and every detail mattered. He'd get Horatio, one of the police officers assigned to help him with the investigation, to pull records. The word of one mattered—if they were willing to talk about it now after all these years of what felt like failed justice.

Her arms wrapped around him, and she clung tightly. "I feel like he's light-years ahead of us."

"He's not. But he is clever." Duke had been cautious about being followed by a car. Not a souped-up truck. It was possible he'd missed it. Or he needed to give this killer reluctant credit—that it was possible the killer knew he had live victims and was now watching and waiting and expecting Duke and Brigitte to figure

it out. How could he not? He was leaving former items of jewelry behind on bodies.

The Sunrise killer either thought he was invincible, and the jewelry was his way of taunting law enforcement, or there was another motive.

Brigitte broke the hold and slowly made her way to Faith Roswell. She closed her eyes and held her hand. "I'm sorry this happened, but I promise, I'm not going to stop until we catch him and put him away forever." She retrieved her cell phone. "No signal. Like I suspected."

"Let me see if I can get this side-by-side going. I'm not taking any chances on him coming in here first."

Brigitte shivered and used her phone to take photos of Faith, since they couldn't call out a crime scene tech yet. Duke pushed the UTV away from the mountain and cranked the engine.

It rolled over a few times and died.

He tried two more times, and on the last try it revved to life. Now to hope they could get back to Faith's without being ambushed. Then they could call the Gran Valle police. Duke turned them around and cautiously drove back toward the open desert.

Taking Brigitte's hand, he breathed a prayer for protection.

Because he wasn't able to see around the mountain, and his blind spot created a perfect place for a killer to lie in wait.

Twenty-four hours had passed since Faith Roswell had been murdered by the man who'd attacked her years before. Brigitte wouldn't be convinced it was anyone else. After making it out of the desert, they'd called the police and the coroner, then salvaged the sketch. She

wouldn't let Faith's courageous act be in vain. Decades had passed and she'd kept that horrible night bottled up, isolating herself in the desert.

While it might not be Brigitte's fault, the weight of people being hurt or murdered because a killer wanted her dead hung around her neck like a heavy noose. This morning, Brigitte and Duke had gone to the precinct to try and pull records of women who had filed a report of an assault that included waking in the desert and being strangled. They searched a large radius and went back about two years prior to Faith's attack.

Her composite showed a very young man. One just beginning to act out his sordid fantasy but not quite able to take a human life, but he'd clearly overcome that hesitation over the years, perfecting his MO and signature—outwitting the police and taunting them with his game of taking and leaving jewelry.

"Hey, Brig," Duke said, "you ready?"

Today they were taking Dad into the Chisos Mountains surrounding Big Bend National Park to the stone cabin where he had proposed to Mom. The cabin had been rented, but they could take a picture in front of it for posterity.

"Almost." She needed to grab the photo album of his and Mom's yearly trip. The box with that album was upstairs in the attic. Each time they made this journey, he'd recorded it with a Polaroid photo. She hoped she was doing the right thing by taking him. Not taking him kept him agitated, and her hope was being in the mountains would calm him. But Mom wasn't there, so she couldn't be sure. The nurse on duty this morning had told her he was well today. She thanked God for the grace and gift of lucidity.

After going up in the attic and retrieving the album and the wicker picnic basket, she grabbed the newer-model instant camera—thankful Polaroids had come back in style. "Food is in the cooler. We can put it in the basket when we get there. Keep things fresh. Let's pray my dad stays lucid. Is this a bad idea?"

Duke grabbed the handle of the cooler on rollers and laid a hand on Brigitte's shoulder. He looked great in khaki cargos, a T-shirt and the hiking boots he'd purchased—though he'd griped about not having broken them in and getting blisters. "Brig, you have to have some normalcy in all this chaos. We'll be up in Big Bend, and you haven't told anyone that's where we'll be except Mrs. Kipling—who sounds a lot like my grandma. I miss her."

She swallowed. That wasn't exactly true. She'd told Ray when she saw him early this morning walking the dog. Things had been patched up, and Brigitte could use an extra eye on the house or a lookout for strange vehicles or men walking by that normally didn't, but Duke suspected him, so she kept that to herself. "I didn't know mine. Or I don't remember them well. We have so much work to do. I need to do the age progression drawing, and we still have reports to comb through." She wasn't going to feel guilty for not working, but Faith's lifeless eyes haunted her. "Any hits?" she asked as she locked up.

"One woman, Denise Govern, went to the police a year before Faith Roswell said she was attacked. She was going in her apartment. He took her to the desert. But no strangulation reported. Unfortunately, Denise ended her life six months after, so we can't speak to her. I called her sister, who is her last living relative. She

said Denise died the day of the attack, it was just her body that died by suicide. She did tell her parents and sister what happened, but no mention of strangulation. Though she did note that a man had followed her. So that jibes with the stalking. She'd been pretty bloody. She fought hard, bless her."

Brigitte's knees turned to water, and blood drained from her face.

*"Brigitte, go to your room. Don't come out until I tell you to. Do you understand?"*

*Red covered Dad's shirt. His face was pale and his eyes wild like a scared dog's.*

*The TV blared. Dad was watching a cop show, and the sirens were loud. So loud. Blaring. "Turn down the TV, Daddy."*

*"In your room."*

*A banging on the door.*

*"Now, Brigitte Ann Linsey!"*

*Brigitte ran to her room and put a pillow over her head.*

She snapped out of the memory.

"You okay over there?"

"Yeah, I just got that memory again. Only this time… I remember being scared and maybe police at my home. I don't know." She didn't want to think about it. She wanted—needed—a peaceful day with her dad. And having Duke with her was a bonus. Brigitte felt safe with him, but then, they'd never discussed that almost kiss, so there was another kind of fear nipping at her conscience. She didn't want to think about that, either.

They drove in comfortable silence to Sunny Days.

"Want me to wait out here?"

"No, Dad needs to see you again, especially if we're

gonna be spending the day together." If it wasn't coming on the heels of everything ominous and uncertain in her life, she'd be way more excited about a day in Big Bend with Duke.

She parked her Jeep near the front entrance, and they were blasted with chilled air and the scents of bleach and lemons as they entered and were greeted by staff.

"Hey, while we're here, you want to meet Mrs. Kipling?" Mrs. Kipling had been vocal about the mystery man, and she might as well be introduced. Plus, it might bring back warm memories of his own grandmother he'd just said he missed.

"Yeah, I'd like that."

She knocked on her door and heard her call to enter.

Mrs. Kipling was wearing a peach tracksuit, and her purse was on her lap.

"It's me, and I brought a friend," Brigitte said. "You going somewhere?"

"Oh, well, what a treat. I didn't think I'd be seeing you today—pardon the pun." Mrs. Kipling had such a positive outlook on her blindness. Never let it keep her down. "And I am going to get my hair set. Vance should be here shortly. He's having a good day with his feet. We might even have some lunch together after."

"That sounds wonderful. I'd like you to meet Special Agent Duke Jericho. We're working on the Sunrise Serial Killer case together." She'd omitted the personal attacks, though the news had run a few segments. Hopefully, Mrs. Kipling wouldn't be too worried and was unaware of the news.

"So pleased to meet you, hon."

Duke grinned and stepped up, taking the hand she

had held out. "My pleasure, ma'am. Brigitte speaks with great affection for you."

Her smile widened, and she patted the top of his hand with the other. "Polite and Southern. But not a Texas drawl."

"Good ear. I'm from Mobile originally. Lived there until I went to the FBI Academy."

"I can tell Brigitte is in capable hands." She gave one last squeeze and released him.

Duke smirked. "Yes, ma'am."

"And how is your investigation going?" she asked. "You going to catch this horrible man?"

"That's the plan." Duke's resolute expression gave Brigitte hope that they would get the Sunrise Serial Killer before he got them.

Mrs. Kipling cupped her mouth with her hands and whispered, "I like this one, Brigitte. He's a keeper."

Brigitte wanted to slide under the bed and hide. "Oh…well…we're not… We're just working together."

"Oh, my mistake." Her tone said she hadn't made a mistake at all.

"Well, we should get going. Gonna be a long day. Pray Dad does well."

"You and your daddy are in my prayers daily. And you've been in my daily prayers, too, Agent Jericho."

"Please call me Duke."

"I do—in my prayers." She snickered. "You kids go on now."

Brigitte hugged Mrs. Kipling, and they slipped into the hall.

"I can't remember the last time someone called me a kid."

"You going to have a big four-oh party next month?" Brigitte slowed as she neared Dad's bedroom.

"If going to work all day then likely ordering pizza could be considered a big four-oh party." He held the door for her.

Duke not celebrating a milestone birthday seemed sad.

"I'm sure Vera will bring me a cupcake against my wishes."

"Vera. Are you two…?"

"No. We're colleagues and friends. I haven't dated anyone since my divorce."

But he'd almost kissed her. Had he almost kissed anyone else? She wasn't daring to ask. It was like he wanted to forget it. Pretend it never happened. She'd go along. What else was she supposed to do?

Dad was dressed and ready to go, standing by the windows that revealed the view of the little park. He turned when they entered. "Brigitte, honey. You look beautiful."

Lucid. Her stomach settled and her nerves relaxed. "Hey, Dad. Thanks. Do you remember Duke Jericho? A friend of mine?" She didn't want to upset him with the talk of homicide and FBI agents.

He stepped forward and shook Duke's hand. "Can't say I do, but a friend of Brigitte's is a friend of mine. Nice to meet you. Ward Linsey."

"Nice to meet you. I heard you proposed at Big Bend."

"Oh, indeed. Let me tell you why." As they signed out and made their way to the Jeep, Dad shared the story of proposing to Mom set against the gorgeous Chisos Mountains. Duke appeared relaxed and to enjoy

Dad's conversation and company. She'd always imagined bringing the one home to meet Dad and that it would go almost perfectly—like now.

But Dad wouldn't know the one in Brigitte's life. He was deteriorating every day.

She wasn't going to let those thoughts consume her. Not today when it was beautiful and Dad was remembering.

Today she wasn't letting the bad in. It was going to be normal and good for once.

She hoped.

# TEN

"You can see why I picked here to propose, can't you, Brigitte?" Dad threw his arm around her shoulders as they gazed upon the glorious Chisos Mountains.

They'd driven the seven-mile-long paved road that climbed into the Chisos Mountains Basin, a little valley ringed by craggy peaks. They'd bypassed the Chisos Mountains Lodge and its dining room that revealed the greatest view of the national park in all of Texas and opted for a picnic to recreate the atmosphere of Ward's proposal.

Here in the basin, even with eighty-nine-degree temps, they were shaded by Douglas fir, Arizona cypress, aspens and maples, and Ponderosa pine. "I don't remember Mom being a hiker." Dad had been. He'd loved to photograph scenery. Maybe he was an artist, just in a different way. Brigitte hadn't thought of that before.

"Oh, she wasn't, but she did feel at peace surrounded by nature. We came up here as kids, and they were some of her happiest times. That's why I proposed here."

They hiked around to the stone cabin where he'd dipped on a bended knee and pledged forever. Brigitte

and her dad led the charge, while Duke brought up the rear, a backpack on his back and toting the picnic basket. He and Dad had talked fishing, photography and of course football on the drive. Brigitte had relished every second and was thrilled Duke was able to know—if even just a glimpse—her real father before his decline.

"That's it. That's the one!" Dad pointed at the small cluster of stone cottages with terra-cotta roofing. "On the end. We honeymooned there."

"A beautiful view of the mountains, Dad."

Sorrow filled his eyes, but he said nothing.

"I have the album. And the camera. We could take a photo together."

Dad smiled and nodded. "I'd like that."

"I'll take the picture," Duke said while dropping the supplies and grabbing the camera. "Been a while since I took a Polaroid." He chuckled, and Brigitte followed Dad to the spot, with the gorgeous mountains behind them, the cabin to the left and beautiful trees shading them.

Dad stood to the right of Brigitte and put his arm around her. "You put your arm around my waist."

Brigitte complied and leaned in, her head almost resting on his shoulder. She'd seen this album more than once a year and had the pose memorized—Mom with her close-lipped smile and Dad beaming, his arm hugging her to him.

"Say cheese," Duke said once they were in position.

"Cheese!" they said in unison, and Duke hit the button. She heard the zip of the Polaroid taking the picture, and then it slid out all foggy. Duke waved it, and the picture developed. They all huddled and stared at it.

"You look like Mary. Where is Mary?" Dad asked.

Brigitte's heart sank. It had been such a great day. They'd taken in the scenery and admired the birds. He'd wholly been her dad and now…now he was confused, and she hoped it didn't cause a meltdown.

"Mary isn't here right now. How about we have a picnic and wait on her?" What was the point in reminding him she was dead? He'd just forget in a short period anyway and have to relive her dying. It was easier to slip into the fantasy.

"Oh, okay."

Duke pulled the blanket from the backpack and spread it on the ground, then Brigitte helped Dad sit before laying out the food and drink. Duke handed Dad the album and the photo.

"Thought you might like to put the picture inside yourself."

"Yes. You're a good man." He cocked his head and frowned. "I can't seem to recall your name."

"Duke," he said patiently.

"Duke. You like to fish?"

"I certainly do. How about you?" He sat next to Dad, and Brigitte could cry at Duke's sweetness. They'd already talked fishing in depth just two hours ago.

Dad flipped open the album and turned the pages. "Isn't she beautiful?"

Duke glanced at Brigitte. "She absolutely is."

Brigitte's insides fluttered, and she handed him a ham and cheese on white bread. Duke gave thanks for the meal, and they ate in comfortable silence. Dad had placed the new photo in the album and was content to enjoy his corned beef on rye.

A breeze rustled the maple leaves, and Brigitte lay

on her back, looking up. Time to imagine and find pictures in the clouds. "You see that one?"

Duke shielded his eyes and followed her line of sight. "Yep."

"What do you see?"

"Hmm…"

A sonic boom cut the atmosphere and the picnic basket blew off the blanket. Brigitte grabbed Dad and yanked him down. "Shooter!"

"Head behind the cabins!" Duke shouted.

"Dad, stay low and with me." He seemed dazed and confused, but he was compliant as they began running and when another bullet hit the ground beside his feet, as if the shooter wasn't aiming to kill but to frighten and toy with Dad.

"What's happening? We need to find Mary! She's in trouble. We can't leave her!"

Now was not the time! "She's safe," Brigitte said, her breath shallow as they ran for the brush to help them find cover.

Another shot nearly missed Duke. "No time to get to the cabins. Duck behind the brush."

Brigitte shoved Dad to the ground and landed on his back, shielding him. Duke dived next to them. "Duke, what do we do?"

"We have to make sure your dad stays safe. Our only chance is to go farther into the park, where we're hidden by trees and the mountains, and hope for the best."

"That sounds pretty slight."

"You got a better option?" he countered.

*No.* Dad kept babbling about the album and Mary. The gunfire wouldn't cease and felt closer. Brigitte couldn't focus.

"I just have to…" Dad bucked Brigitte from his back and bolted from the brush straight toward the shooter. "I gotta get the album! Our memories!"

The whole world slanted, and Brigitte froze for a split second, then sprang from the brush, but Duke had already reacted and was chasing down Dad. Brigitte pursued. She couldn't cower and let two people she cared about be murdered by some revengeful killer.

A bullet split the dirt next to Dad, and he covered his head and flinched. Duke dived onto him, toppling him to the ground, and Dad fought back, swinging. No one was going to keep him from that album. Duke wouldn't hurt Dad, but he had to get him under control to save him.

Brigitte shot past them, a bullet hitting too close to home, and snatched the album, then rolled down the hill like the area was burning, losing a tennis shoe in the process.

Duke had Dad in a bear hug, leg wrapped around his to pin him from kicking and arms holding his down to keep Dad from hitting, and they began to roll with Brigitte down the brush-laden hill. Rocks dug into her back and something sharp pinched her leg. Like a carnival ride without a seat belt, she tumbled until she rolled into tree with a thud that snapped her teeth together.

She lay there trying to regain her breath, then remembered Dad and Duke. She rolled onto her belly but didn't see them. "Duke! Dad!"

"Over here," Duke called.

The pinch in her leg was a long cactus needle. She slowly removed it, wincing at the pain, then slithered on her belly through brush and dirt until she found Duke

lying on his back and Dad in a fetal position crying and mumbling Mom's name.

So much for a peaceful day.

The gunshots ceased. "He can't find us or he's changing position," Duke whispered.

Brigitte curled up beside Dad. "I have the album."

He took it and clutched it to his chest. "I want to go home."

"Me, too, Dad. Me, too."

The roar of an engine at the top of the hill sent another wave of adrenaline through her, but a park ranger peered over, identifying herself as Salome Rivera. Duke called out who they were and that they'd been shot at.

"Calls came in. Several more of us up here. Can you make it up the hill?"

"Are you sure we're safe?" Brigitte asked.

"I think we scared him off. We've got rangers on horses moving into the area now."

Duke sighed, and Brigitte helped Dad up. "Let's go home, Dad."

"I want Mary."

"Me, too."

"You okay?" Duke handed her the lost shoe.

She nodded then shook her head. Words wouldn't come.

"I just want to go home, Duke."

After giving a report, they packed it up and drove Dad back to Sunny Days. Brigitte made sure Dad was safe and resting, then she and Duke walked outside. The sky had turned dark, and a rumble of thunder broke through the clouds. "I need a minute." Brigitte walked to the park and collapsed on a bench. A drop of rain

plopped on her cheek, cooling her flushed skin, but she couldn't care less about rain.

Duke sat quietly beside her.

"I feel like I'm in a nightmare I can't wake up from. You know, a lot of times, I can wake myself up out of a bad dream, but this…this feels like it's not ever going to end, but keep getting worse until everyone around me is ash and I'm six feet under. I can't stop it. I can't fix it. I can't… I just can't. Dad could have died today. And it was my fault. A stupid idea."

She leaned forward, her hair covering her face as thunder cracked and a light drizzle misted them. But Duke didn't seem to mind. She stood and ran her hands through her hair, then sighed and turned to look at him.

He perched on the bench, studying her, his eyes a mixture of concern and something she couldn't quite identify. No one had ever looked at her like that before. It was intense and piercing, sending a spray of flutters inside her chest.

"Tell me I'm going to wake up," she whispered. In some ways she felt very awake now. Her skin flushed hot, and her throat turned dry.

Duke slowly stood and closed the two feet of distance between then. He slid damp hair from her face and tucked it behind her ear, and in that moment, she realized going weak in the knees wasn't cliché but a true description—she'd just never experienced it before. Gazing into his eyes, she blinked away raindrops dotting her eyelashes.

Duke's hair was damp and beginning to curl around his brow and ears. "You're going to wake up. There will be an end. You had an overall good day, and your

father is fine. Didn't even seem fazed by the time we got back."

Without thought, she fell against his chest, the words comforting her and allowing her to lean in and depend. He'd almost kissed her once. Never spoke of it. Brigitte had chalked it up to rejection, but his eyes, his actions… could he be afraid of his feelings? She was. They'd come hard and fast and without warning. Unexpected but full of bright color. Like light to a dark canvas.

She gazed up at him, arrested in his eyes, and then he slowly descended on her lips. Wet from rain, warm and welcoming. His hands slid into her hair as he expertly tasted her lips. Her head turned fuzzy, and pops of color danced along her senses. He was soft blues that brought comfort and powerful red that knew how to wield a kiss without fear or hesitation. Gold and warm. Green like new hope and life. White and pure. She felt like royal purple the way he respected, admired and cherished her. Her heart rose like an orange sunrise.

She lost her breath in the slow-measured kiss, ignoring the increase in rain. Nothing could stop this connection. Not a raging storm. Not a killer in the shadows. Not even fear, because in this kiss—all fear was lost. All hope was found.

She felt alive and awake. Like she hadn't even known she'd been sleeping.

Finally, when they'd lost their breath and their lungs demanded oxygen, Duke gently broke the kiss, inhaled and pecked her nose and her forehead, then rested his brow against hers. "I've never met anyone like you, Brigitte."

"And I've never met anyone like you."

So what did this mean? By now her clothes were

drenched and her hair plastered to her head. She glanced up, shielding the rain from her eyes, and he grinned, then she did. They were in the middle of a storm kissing. Like something out of movie. Then they were laughing together, and he grabbed her hand and they darted into the parking lot and to the Jeep.

They sat in their seats, water drenching the leather and rain beating on the vehicle. They remained quiet. Listening.

What was he thinking? The air crackled with tension, and she suddenly felt like an idiot. "Did you say you were going to make a call to Kayla Lowe's friend?" She blurted and broke the silence, turning it back to the case, because she wasn't sure what else to do, if he rejected her and after that kiss, she'd probably puddle into a lost cause in her seat.

He cleared his throat. "Did I? I need to."

She cranked the engine and turned the air off so they wouldn't get a chill.

"Then let's pursue that lead next."

"Is that all you want to pursue, Brigitte?"

Duke stared into Brigitte's eyes and didn't mistake the fear and trepidation he saw there. Everything in his gut screamed *run* as his reasons for not pursuing a relationship played on a continuous loop in his head.

Except when he was kissing her.

When he'd ignored his brain and led with his heart, there was no hesitation in kissing her. The moment his lips had connected with hers, it had been like an explosion in his head. Not due to her softness, her eagerness or the taste of her. But the vulnerability mixed with the confidence of a woman who knew how to give and not

simply be a taker. And that was Brigitte in everything she did. Gave and gave. Rarely taking and sometimes having to be reminded that she did need to receive help, encouragement and a strong place to lean.

Duke had been there once, too. He recognized the signs. He'd wanted no help. No support. Duke had shouldered everything, and that had been a huge part in his marriage ending. And when he'd been reminded he needed to do those things, unlike Brigitte, he'd balked and gotten defensive.

Brigitte's pause made his gut clench. "I'm sorry. That's an unfair question to ask. You're emotional and spent. I was out of line."

"No," she said, "you weren't. I am emotional and I am spent, but I'm not deluded or unable to process. I just… I'm scared. And things are crazy. It's hard to think about normalcy—like kisses and dates. I don't know if I'll even—if I'll even be alive tomorrow—"

"You will," he said with more force than intended. Because the thought of Brigitte not in this world, in his life, was more than he wanted to consider. "I'm not letting anything happen to you."

She touched his face. "I've learned there are no certainties in life, Duke. A lot of it is out of our control. I trust God, but I'm certainly not going to presume that just because I trust Him, He won't allow me to die. Otherwise believers would never die." She chuckled, but he felt every ounce of sorrow in it.

"Then let me rephrase. I'm going to do everything I can to keep you safe," he said.

"That I believe."

"How about we discuss it when things blow over?

See where we land. And until then, let's not confuse ourselves any further."

Light dimmed in her eyes, and she dropped her hand from his face. "Okay."

Had he said something wrong? So much for being less confused. They finished their drive back to Brigitte's in squirmy silence. After clearing the house, Duke retired to his bedroom to put on dry clothes. About ten minutes later, he heard Brigitte stirring, then the teakettle whistled. He got the feeling she needed some alone time. He certainly did.

It wasn't that he didn't trust God. God had been faithful. God had helped comfort him in his darkest days. Duke didn't trust relationships and maybe women. Maybe himself. And he wasn't sure he could take another hit to his heart. He raked a hand through his hair and let out a frustrated sigh, then picked up his Bible, which always gave him peace.

Footsteps creaked the joists outside his room, then a door opened and closed. Brigitte was in the room next to him. He read and listened as the sounds of drawers opening and closing came, footsteps tracked across the room. Should he go in there? Keep giving her space? He continued to read, but the noise was distracting.

Brigitte was distracting. Everything he didn't want. The very reason he'd hesitated when she'd asked to work with him. But she was efficient and smart. He had to admit he enjoyed working with her. Enjoyed being here in her house, which felt like a home. Not just her childhood home, but she'd made it hers with the bright colors and art.

The shrill timbre of her cell phone snapped him out of his thoughts. Her muffled voice spoke frantically,

then he heard her footfalls on the stairs. Duke met her in the living room, her face a mixture of torment and frustration. "Dad's having an episode—like we should be surprised—and they want me to come. See if I can calm him. Sometimes I can. Sometimes I can't. More than half the time he doesn't remember me."

"Why don't you let me drive?" he offered. She nodded and trailed behind him into the kitchen, where they grabbed their guns and he snagged the keys to her Jeep. He hit the garage door button, and they hopped inside her car and headed for Sunny Days again. The rain had slackened, but not enough to ignore using the windshield wipers.

Back at the assisted living center, Duke followed Brigitte down the hall and into her dad's room. Two nurses were trying to talk him down, but Ward was combative and it appeared he'd been crying. Today had been too much, and the danger he'd been in had sent him spiraling. Watching this scene tore him up, and he glanced at Brigitte. For a brief moment, her eyes filled with moisture, but then her cop face replaced it. Calm. Collected. In control.

But he knew inside she was a downpour of emotion.

"Dad," she murmured, "it's Brigitte."

Ward paused, the album open beside him, and stared at Brigitte, then slumped near his bed. "I'm so sorry, Mary. You don't have to leave. How will I care for Brigey-Bear alone?"

Brigitte's chin quivered, and she pushed past the nurses, who seemed more than relieved she was here. She knelt beside him. "Mary isn't leaving."

"She wanted to. So many times. I—I wish I'd been enough. I tried."

Brigitte wrapped her arms around her dad. "But she stayed. She loved you."

Was she humoring him or had Mary Linsey tried to leave her marriage? And if so, why?

"I loved her. I just wish it had been enough. But there was…was so much blood."

Brigitte's jaw clenched, and she laid her head on her father's shoulder. "What blood?"

Duke's insides curled up. He felt like he was intruding on a deeply private moment, but no one had asked him to leave. He slowly picked up the album. Maybe it wasn't today but something in the album, on this page, that had triggered him.

Brigitte suddenly sat up ramrod straight. It sent a chill through Duke.

"Dad, did…did Mary try to hurt herself? In the bathtub?"

Ward Linsey began crying and shaking his head as if he was stuck in the past. Duke glanced down at the four photos, noticing how happy Ward looked, but Mary… Mary didn't have much light in her eyes. And that's when he saw it.

He tried not to gasp, but it was there. Pinned on her left shoulder.

A gold brooch with an emerald-cut ruby.

No. No, surely not. He slipped the photo from the clear plastic protector and turned it over and read the date.

Eighteen years ago. Brigitte would have been ten years old. She said she was about that age when she remembered her dad painting and his hands red. But that wasn't paint, Duke feared.

He flipped through the earlier photos but didn't see

the brooch, then he flipped through the rest of them. No brooch.

"The blood was everywhere. I didn't know what to do." His voice began to rise, and he became agitated again. "I couldn't help her, and I'm just so sorry."

"She's okay. Mary's okay," Brigitte said. "How about I help you into your chair and you can watch *M\*A\*S\*H*?"

"I like that show. Alan Alda is a fine actor."

"Yeah, I know." She helped him up, her eyes tired and face pale. She'd been trying to take care of everyone, handle all her dad's affairs and work a grueling job. At some point, exhaustion was going to get her.

Once Ward was settled in his recliner and calm, Brigitte talked with the nurses and she and Duke left the assisted living center. Duke had the photo album, but he wasn't sure how to tell Brigitte that her mother might have also been an early victim of the Sunrise Serial Killer. That the reason that brooch triggered her wasn't just to open up a repressed memory about blood because the gem was a ruby, but that deep in her subconscious she'd recognized that piece of jewelry. Every time she looked at this album with her dad…she saw it. She'd either forgotten or hadn't paid it attention, but either way, in the deep recesses of her mind—she remembered.

Duke didn't have the heart to add one more bomb on her tonight. She'd already been the victim of a literal one. She needed rest. They both did, and when she'd had some, he'd break his suspicions to her. She now suspected her mom had wanted to end her life. The attack had to have been after their trip—she was wearing the brooch—but before Brigitte turned eleven, so pretty soon after that photo was taken. It had been too

much, and it appeared Mary Linsey had tried to end it. Just like their other victim, Denise Govern, who had survived the assault.

As they approached Brigitte's home, she sighed. "I think my mother tried to end her life that night. I think what I heard was real officers, not a TV show, and I think I suppressed the memory. But I don't know what triggered Dad to keep thinking about it or why I remembered it by looking at that brooch."

Duke changed his mind. She needed to know. Brigitte would never sleep anyway. Too much on her mind.

He reached his arm back to the floorboard and picked up the album he'd taken from the home. Brigitte hadn't even noticed. "You need to look at this."

"What am I looking for?"

He came to the stop sign and found the photo, then pointed to it. "That," he murmured.

A garbled sob came from her throat. "No," she said as she shook her head. "That was my mother's…she was…"

The dam broke when he pulled into her driveway, and he drew her close to him. "We don't know anything for certain."

"We know he takes jewelry from victims and places them on new ones. Kayla was the new victim. I don't remember ever seeing it on my mom or in her jewelry box. Not even before this picture. But she must have had it, and he took it when he brutalized her." She raised her head up, her eyes hollow and wide. "That's why she hurt herself in the bathtub. Like Denise Govern, who reported her assault but killed herself six months later." Slowly she put the same pieces together that Duke had on the way here.

"I'm so sorry, Brigitte." It didn't feel like enough.

"Do you think he took the brooch from the scene because he quickly connected me to it? Couldn't be sure if I'd have recognized it or not and in a snap decision snatched it back?"

"I think he knew his prints were on it."

"Cards. Do…do you think he left her anniversary cards like the others?" Her face turned ashen, and she jumped from the Jeep and got sick in the bushes.

He helped her inside and guided her to her bathroom. "Take a shower and breathe. We will figure this out. If it's true, we will get this guy."

For now they both needed rest, even when it was the last thing either of them wanted. They couldn't afford to be sluggish.

Not when the Sunrise Serial Killer had his sights set on Brigitte.

# ELEVEN

Brigitte had tossed and turned all night long. Something niggled at the edges of her memory. Something key, but it wouldn't come, and after last night there was no way she could bring it up to Dad. On a bad day it would only make things worse, and on a good day it could trigger him and send him down a slippery slope.

She was on her own. Unless Ray had information that Dad trusted him to never tell or he hadn't thought it was her place to know—or maybe Ray thought she did know her family's history.

But her gut said she was missing some crucial pieces. The thought of her mother a victim of the Sunrise Serial Killer... It roiled her stomach and shot acid into her throat, leaving her light-headed and nauseated. She hadn't been able to eat much of the breakfast Duke had cooked them before coming to the Gran Valle police station. It was so weird working out of a station she didn't technically work for.

They'd hit a dead end with the classmates David Hyatt had given them. Today they were going to talk to Kayla's friend Cheyenne West, who lived in El Paso. She was coming to collect a few boxes from Kayla's

sister that belonged to her, and they planned to meet at the station for questioning and so Brigitte could draw a composite of the man Cheyenne had seen Kayla getting into a car with.

She hoped it would match the younger drawing. Something about the eyes seemed familiar to her. She couldn't place it. Maybe she just wanted it to be familiar so she could catch the killer. Right now, with old memories, she couldn't be sure of anything.

She left the interview room and bumped right into Will. "Hey."

"Hey, I was coming to look for you," he said and dug his phone out of his pocket.

Brigitte's stomach knotted. "Why?"

"Patricia had the baby late last night. I got a picture." He held out the phone, and she leaned in to see. Will and Terry had grown up together and remained friends. That's how she'd met Will—through Terry and Patricia.

Patricia holding a precious little babe in her arms, and Terry was in a sling and a wheelchair, grinning from ear to ear, as if he'd never been shot and almost lost his life and would be on desk duty forever.

"It's a boy. They named him James Wheaton. I think they're gonna call him Wheaton. Patricia's maiden name. It's weird, huh?" He chuckled, and she grinned.

"Nah, I like it. It'll fit him. No doubt he'll be blond like his parents."

"I got a few more. Don't tell anyone, but I'm kind of a sucker for babies." He scrolled through several more photos, and Brigitte longed for that—a family of her own. But she wasn't ready to risk being that vulnerable or taking that chance.

"Me, too. I'd want a house full of them."

"Really?" He cocked his head. "I got the impression you wanted to paint. Be alone. I mean, you never really gave me a reason—other than caring for your dad— why we broke up. I thought it was an excuse not to get serious with me."

It had been. "I'm not good in long-term relationships. I just… I don't want one. But if I did, then I'd want a lot of kids. That's what I meant."

"I get it. Sort of." He shrugged.

"Let me see those baby pictures again." Leaning in, she studied the happy family as Will kept scrolling, and they chatted about baby stuff and how Terry was doing. "I'll take her a meal once she gets home. See the baby." Apologize a hundred times again. Hold the baby and be thankful he had a daddy in his life.

A throat cleared, and she pivoted. Duke stood at the corner of the hall. "Cheyenne West is here. She got into town early."

"Oh. Great."

Will glanced at Duke, then turned to Brigitte. "You want me to let them know you'll be by in a few days? I'm going over there later."

"Yeah. That'd be great. Thanks. Give the baby a kiss for me."

"Patricia won't let anyone kiss the baby. Air kisses." He winked and saluted, then jetted toward the bullpen.

"She's in the lobby," Duke said. "I'll get her." His eyes were narrowed and his jaw clenched.

"Everything okay?"

"Yeah. Yeah, it's all good." He turned, and she frowned. Something wasn't good. She hurried inside the conference room and retrieved her sketch pad and pencils.

In a few moments, Duke held the door open for a knockout redhead. He introduced them, then offered Cheyenne a seat.

"What can you tell us about that day you saw Kayla get into the car with the older man?" Brigitte asked. She wanted to recreate the scene in Cheyenne's mind so when it came time to recall his features, she'd be in the moment.

Cheyenne tucked a long, wavy lock behind her ear. "Kayla had been noticeably happier, and she didn't go to dinner much anymore after art class. We teased her about having a new man in her life, but she was pretty vague, like she didn't want anyone to know. The day I saw him pick her up, she was rushing and forgot her sketch pad. I ran after her, calling, and she ignored me. I figured out why when I saw him."

"Why was that?"

"He was considerably older than her, and she probably didn't want us to pick at her about it." She grinned. "And we would have, of course. Why is it men age better than women?"

Brigitte snickered. "I have no idea. Feels unfair. When you say pick at her…you mean teasing in fun, right?"

"Well, sure, but also, I mean personally…while silver foxes may look good…when she's forty-five, he's, like, seriously geriatric. Is that mean?"

*Yes. Completely.* "It's your opinion, and everyone is entitled to theirs. Did Kayla know how you felt about dating older men?" That might be why she dashed away—not because she was hiding an older man, but she didn't want to hear Cheyenne's opinion.

Duke shifted in his chair, remaining quiet and un-

comfortable. But he'd been distracted earlier. She wished she knew why.

"She did. Someone mentioned our art teacher, David, was a looker, and a few jokes were murmured. I said I'd never date anyone past five years older than me because I didn't want to deal with being saddled…well, never mind what I said. Point is, she knew."

Seemed selfish. Marriage was for better or worse. And what about young couples where one ended up needing around-the-clock care? No, Brigitte was not a fan of Cheyenne and her opinion. "I see. What did his car look like?"

"Flashy and navy blue or black. Four-door. Maybe a Benz. I can't say for sure. I was looking at her and then him. He had on sunglasses. Aviators, I believe. Kinda reminded me of Richard Gere before he went all silver. Same protruding nose that's bulbous at the end, and thick lips."

Brigitte worked not to actually draw Richard Gere. But now he was in her head. *Ugh.* "Chin?"

"Oh, wow. I mean, not squared but not like a moon shape." She cringed. "Sorry. I'm bad at description, apparently."

"You're doing fine."

She held up a finger as if a lightbulb had gone off. "Oh! He had a clean-shaven face, and his arms were defined and tanned. One was resting on the open window as she rushed, and he waved at her."

"Helpful. What kind of hair did he have?"

"Thick. Full. Black with graying temples and pops of silver throughout. Cut short and trendy above his ears." She'd said he was fit, so Brigitte worked to de-

fine his jaw in the sketch. "Do you think I can identify her killer? Does that, like, put me in danger?"

Based on Brigitte's track record with the killer? Affirmative. "We don't know for certain this man is the killer. Did you call after her or anything that would have gotten his attention?"

"No. I stood about twenty feet away and watched. I was surprised." She drummed her perfectly painted peach nails on the conference table with one hand and toyed with her hair with the other. "Once she was in the car, he kissed her."

Hmm…didn't feel like taunting behavior. Some of the other victims had been married or were in a relationship at the time of their deaths. So this guy inserting himself as a love interest didn't jibe. Either way, they needed to discover his identity. He could have pertinent information.

She shaded and shaped and sketched as the description came into view. Instead of drawing eyes, she drew aviator shades, then stared at the sketch before holding it up to Cheyenne, who nodded emphatically. "That's him. That's the guy."

Brigitte's pulse spiked, and she glanced at Duke, who had remained unusually quiet. Now, he stood. "Thank you for coming in and all your help. If you think of anything else, please call." He handed her his business card, and she tucked it in her purse and left.

"What do you think?" Duke pointed to the composite.

She studied her drawing. "I know this man. But I can't place him. The sunglasses are throwing me off." It was there. All Brigitte had to do was allow her mind

to recall him. "Speaking of being thrown off, what's going on with you? I know something is on your mind."

Duke heaved a breath. "It is, but I don't think here in the interview room is the time or the place."

Brigitte's stomach knotted. Felt like a breakup to her. They weren't together officially, but that kiss...that had been something more than physical attraction. At least on her part. Maybe she'd dreamed up their instant connection and the feelings of it maturing. She so badly wanted someone to understand her, to bond with her. Had she imagined it?

"Right. Later, then." She collected her things and picked up the composite. "I'm going to have flyers made." She headed for the door.

"Wait."

Brigitte turned. Duke's eyes had darkened, and he pointed at the composite. "Put a pair of sunglasses on the art gallery owner. Raphe LaMont."

Taking another look at the composite, she didn't have to imagine it. Raphe owned a pair of aviator-style Ray-Ban sunglasses. He did have a Richard Gere appearance with a little more pronounced nose and less squinty eyes, but Cheyenne wouldn't have known that due to the glasses.

Blood drained from her face. "You're right. It's Raphe."

"The note on the card from the florist to Kayla was signed R, too. What do you know about him and Mina?"

Brigitte pinched the bridge of her nose. "They moved to El Paso from LA twenty years ago or so to help build up the smaller art communities. But they'd had connections here for much longer. Raphe is originally from El Paso. They still have ties to big galleries in LA and New York."

"I'd like to know if any attacks like this happened in deserts near LA. I'll get one of our FBI analysts on it." He retrieved his cell phone from his suit pocket. "In the meantime, I'd like to have a chat with Raphe about Kayla."

So would Brigitte. Debbie Deardon could be connected to him. They needed to find out who else.

Duke sat in the passenger seat of Brigitte's Jeep on their way to Los Artes Gallery to talk with Raphe. He lived in the area at the time of the murders. Had access to the victims. He was in the art community. Respected. No one would suspect him. But how did he connect to Brigitte's mom? They had yet to discover a definitive link to all the victims.

While Duke needed to remain focused on the case, his thoughts swept back and forth to Brigitte. Earlier, he'd rounded the corner and saw her with Officer Talbort—a man she'd been in a relationship with before—and they seemed on good terms. She'd been leaning in as they looked at baby pictures. He was closer to Brigitte in age—his knees probably didn't pop when he squatted, and his back was unlikely to be stiff every morning.

Jealousy had left a green streak through him. But what had struck closest to home was Cheyenne West's conversation with Brigitte about older men. True that when Brig was forty-five he'd be almost sixty. Facts threaded with insecurity and fear wrapped around his heart and compressed. Duke wasn't the right guy for her, and pursuing her was selfish and would only hurt them both in the end. But discussing it during work

hours where cameras had been installed was a terrible time and place.

She parked on the side of the street behind a dark four-door Benz. Same kind of car Cheyenne West had described. So far it wasn't looking good for Raphe.

"See what I see?" Brigitte asked.

"Yep."

He followed her inside. The gallery was empty. Duke headed for the offices. "Mr. LaMont."

Voices were muffled behind closed doors. A woman and a man. Brigitte exchanged a look with Duke, and he knocked. The conversation instantly halted and, in a few moments, Raphe opened the door and slipped through, closing it behind him. "Brigitte, Agent Jericho. What brings you to the gallery today? Is it about your painting? It sold. Isn't that wonderful? Congrats."

"Is Mina here?" Brigitte asked.

"No, left this morning to Los Angeles."

His wife was out of town. But behind that door was a woman. A woman who wasn't Raphe's wife.

"I see. Well, we're not here about the painting." She looked to Duke to take the lead.

"We have a witness who can positively ID you. Said that you picked up Kayla Lowe from one of her art classes at Hope Community Center in El Paso. We'd like to know why you kept that information from us when we were here last time." Composites weren't always perfect, but Raphe didn't need to know that was the method of identification. If he balked, the next step was to put him in a lineup with sunglasses on. Hopefully, he'd assume someone he knew had seen him and relayed the information to the authorities.

Raphe glanced at the door and pointed toward a large

room filled with easels, blank canvases stacked against the walls, crates, and two love seats with a coffee table. They entered the room. "Have a seat."

They sat on one love seat, and Raphe perched on the other.

He inhaled. Exhaled. "I didn't say anything about my relationship with Kayla because Mina was standing there."

"But you never offered to call or come forward privately." Duke leaned his elbows on his knees and waited.

Raphe's neck flushed red, and he massaged the back of his neck. "Kayla and I met when she came into the gallery. She was interested in art. Told me she'd been taking a class, and we…we had chemistry. It escalated. Yes, I picked her up a couple of times from her art class."

"What about the flowers sent to her apartment?"

"What about them?" So he had sent them.

"The card?"

His eyes narrowed. "What? A man can't be poetic?" He sat quietly, then those narrow eyes widened and he shook his head vehemently. "Oh, you can't seriously think I killed Kayla or those other women. That's absurd."

"Is it? I don't think so." Duke waited to see what he would do next.

Raphe jumped up, fuming, and threw his hands in the air. "I would never hurt anyone."

"You're hurting your wife with an affair."

His nostrils flared. "Well, that's my personal business, and I'm not murdering Mina."

Murdering her heart. But he was right. That was

his personal business, and Duke wasn't here to judge what he did inside his marriage, though it nauseated him. "Did Kayla mention anything suspicious to you?"

"She didn't say anything, but she acted funny the week before she died. I thought it was in regards to being with a married man. Paranoid. She went from parking outside the flower shop to the little garage behind—it had been a makeshift art studio prior. But after she died, I wondered if she might have known her killer, if she'd been threatened or something."

It was possible. The parking in her garage instead of outside wouldn't have anything to do with the guilt or paranoia of having an affair but hiding from someone or keeping them out of her car. For now, this was all they had. They couldn't hold him on suspicion or arrest him for being a terrible husband. "Where were you the weekend Kayla went missing?"

Raphe cleared his throat. "I was with a friend that weekend, hiking in Big Bend. I enjoy going up there. Having a meal at the lodge and enjoying the view."

That wasn't far from where they'd been shot at. Was he toying with them? "I'll need that name."

"Angela Wreston." He gave Duke her phone number.

Duke stood. "She who's in the office? I can ask now."

"No. She and Kayla aren't the only women I have or had a relationship with."

"You're shooting fast and loose with the word *relationship*," Brigitte muttered, and Duke held in his grin.

"Well, quite frankly, Brigitte, your opinion doesn't matter. I'll have a check cut for your painting later this week. You can pick it up then."

She nodded, and they left the gallery. Inside her Jeep,

she clicked her seat belt in place. "You like him for the Sunrise killer?"

"I don't know. I haven't ruled him out. He's a complete tool, though. Too bad I can't arrest him for that."

"Yeah. I hear ya."

"Unfaithfulness...divorce... It's like someone throws you off a cliff—nothing to cling to, no way to hold on. You just free-fall but you don't die. You land alive, but it knocks the breath from your lungs. You lay there unable to move, panicked inside and clutching your chest. You never think you'll be able to breathe again, and you don't...not for a while. And even then, it takes such a toll and is so traumatic. And that's what I want to talk to you about."

"Unfaithfulness? I may have never stayed in a relationship very long, but I've never cheated."

"No." His gut turned. "All those feelings I just blurted out... I don't plan to ever marry again. I heard you talking to Officer Talbort. About babies. Families. I—I can't give you that, Brigitte. I'm not saying I think you'd be unfaithful. I'm saying that I'm not taking any more risks. I don't have it in me. And if that's not enough, I'm going to be forty next month. You're twenty-eight—recently turned. Did you not hear what Cheyenne West said?"

Brigitte stared at her fingers resting in her lap. She inhaled deeply and cranked the engine. "I understand. I don't want to take a long-term chance, either. I have my reasons. Besides, I really need to focus on my dad right now. He consumes any downtime I have. I don't know how long I have with him physically. Mentally, it's rare. I don't have time for a relationship anyway, certainly not one that's long-distance."

Duke felt the crushing blow as if he hadn't been the one to deal it first. No matter how they spun it, there was no way to make it work. Not without it ending sooner rather than later.

"I'm sorry. I'm attracted to you, Brigitte, and not only physically. I like the way you see the world and people. I admire your kindness and generosity. You think of others. I'm not sorry I kissed you. I wanted to do that. It wasn't a slip in the moment. I'm just sorry I can't make good on what it represented. I do regret that."

She pulled onto the road. "I understand. I need to get back to my house. I want to go through Dad's records. I remember an ambulance at the house, and I also remember her being gone for what felt like a long time. Dad told me she was on a trip to see family. I believed it. But now, I think she was in the hospital for a while because of the self-harm. I want to try and find proof. Like hospital records. See if I can pinpoint a specific date."

There was nothing personal left to say anyway. "Okay. I can help you."

"Sure."

They drove back to her home in silence, cleared the house, then Duke went to work in the attic while Brigitte dug through her father's old home office. He'd gone through an hour's worth of boxes full of documents and receipts but hadn't found any medical records when he heard footsteps below him.

He peeked down through the open attic door.

"I found it. A file with medical records." Brigitte stood holding a manila file folder. "When I was ten, she spent three weeks in the psych ward at Gran Valle General. I don't have any other details. But it's proof that she did try to hurt herself and was committed."

Duke wiped sweat from his brow with the back of his hand. "I'm sorry."

Brigitte's lip quivered. "I didn't want it to be true. But all signs point to the fact that my mother was an early victim when I was a little girl." Tears brimmed in her eyes and spilled onto her cheeks, and while he wanted to run to her and hold her to comfort her, after their earlier conversation, he knew he couldn't.

"How about we go to the hospital and see if we can talk to someone? Is there a doctor listed in that information?"

She shook her head as her cell phone rang. She blew out a heavy breath. "It's Sunny Days." She answered and listened. "I'll be there." She ended the call. "Dad's asking for Mary and a lost engagement ring this time. He's all out of sorts. It's relentless, and he's becoming agitated. I'm afraid I made a mistake taking him to the mountains. On more than one level. I need to see to him. If I can soothe him, they won't have to sedate him. I'll take the album back, too. That might help him see he was married and he doesn't need to find the ring."

They immediately left and drove to Sunny Days. She pulled under the awning. "I'll see to him. You go to the hospital and see what you can find out. Then come back here and pick me up." She opened the driver's door without waiting for him to respond.

Duke jumped behind the wheel and beelined it to Gran Valle General. He headed for Admissions and showed his creds, then asked for some help finding out if the doctor who might have been on the psych ward treating the late Mary Linsey more than a decade ago was still on staff or how Duke could be put in touch with him.

After some teeth pulling and finagling, Duke stepped off the elevator onto the psych ward to meet with Dr. Henry Chambliss, now chief of the psychiatric unit at Gran Valle. But he'd been one of two attending doctors during that time frame and likely treated Mary Linsey.

Dr. Chambliss shook his hand and offered him a seat across from his desk. The man's space was tidy, sparse and full of relaxing blues. Duke explained the situation and showed him the evidence proving Mary Linsey had been in the psych ward here.

"I remember Mary. She'd attempted to end her life. I counseled her. I can confirm that she had been sexually assaulted and she'd felt it was the only way out of the pain, the trauma."

"Did she happen to mention a piece of jewelry he might have taken?"

Dr. Chambliss cocked his head and squinted. "Hold on." He riffled through a huge filing cabinet and retrieved a file. He flipped through it and nodded. "Yes. She did. He took a brooch that had been her grandmother's and was given to her on her sixteenth birthday. Gold with a ruby in the center. He'd called it a token."

So it definitely belonged to Mary. "How long was she hospitalized?"

"She was here three weeks but saw me for about four years. Within that time, we talked about a great many things other than her attack. I'm sorry to hear she passed and that her husband is ill with Alzheimer's. And the daughter?"

"Brigitte. She's…" She's the best thing that had ever entered his life. "She's an artist. Gifted. And a patrol officer with the Los Artes Police Department." He ex-

plained a little more in depth how Brigitte was involved in the case.

Dr. Chambliss removed his wire-rimmed glasses and rubbed his eyes. "That poor child. I'm not surprised she repressed those memories. I imagine seeing her mother like that was traumatic. Mary loved Brigitte, but she was in a bad place for a very long time, and it affected a great many of her relationships. I don't think she ever fully recovered."

"I'm sorry to hear that." Duke couldn't imagine what it must have been like. "We've also found another victim who survived." He told the doctor what Faith Roswell had conveyed before she was gunned down. "Does that sound similar to Mary's story?"

"Almost verbatim, including anniversary cards each year on the attack date. But Mary had been working at the movies. They closed late on Saturday night, and she turned down a ride with a friend since her dad was picking her up. But he got called in to work—she found out later—and when she tried her friend again, he didn't pick up. Her attack happened as she was walking home. She did say—" he referred to Mary's patient file "—that he said her eyes were 'like a lovely star before sunrise.'"

The exact same words Faith Roswell said her attacker told her. That definitely linked both cases but that didn't clear up the confusion pertaining to the rest of the account. "Why was her father picking her up? Seems odd for a grown, married woman."

Now it was Dr. Chambliss's turn to appear confused. "I'm sorry, I assumed you knew. Mary's nonfatal suicide attempt *was* in her late twenties, but it was due to repressed emotions from an attack and assault a week before her eighteenth birthday."

# TWELVE

"Dad, it's Brigitte." Brigitte entered his room as he scoured through dresser drawers, his clothing slung all over his studio-style apartment. Papers littered the floor, books had been tossed aimlessly and even the sheets on his bed and his mattress had been tossed.

"I have to find it! She needs me. Mary needed me, and I wasn't there. But I'm gonna be here for her now. No one will know. No one will know."

Brigitte's insides slumped. *Ah, Dad.* The nurse who'd called her stood by the window, shrugging. "He's determined to find that ring, Miss Linsey. I know you often can talk him down."

Taking a deep, calming breath, Brigitte stepped up to the bed. "You're making too much of a mess to find the ring. I'll help you. Let's be systematic about it." Dad had always told her that same thing when her room had become a disaster as a little girl and she was too overwhelmed to tackle it. Dad was always a logical person.

He stopped for the first time since Brigitte arrived. "That's good advice."

Cloudy eyes stared into hers, awaiting a command. "First tell me why it's so important we find it right now.

Tell me about Mary, and I'll start cleaning up the mess so we can make room to find the ring." Hopefully, she could talk him down and he'd forget the ring—for now.

"Oh, Mary is so beautiful. Smart. She's lived next door to me her whole life, and I've loved her about that long."

Brigitte's heart melted. She knew they'd been neighbors—her dad about four years older than her mother. Brigitte began picking up the strewn pieces of clothing and shoving them back into the drawers where they belonged. "And how long has she loved you?" Brigitte asked and scooped up another pile of shirts.

"Oh, Mary's never loved me. At least…not like I love her."

Brigitte froze. Dad must be confused. Her mother had been distant and aloof, and Brigitte now suspected it was due to depression that led to her suicide attempt, but she'd never thought Mom hadn't loved Dad. "I'm sure she most certainly loves you."

Tears filled his eyes. "No. She turned me down, but now she needs me. And I'm gonna be there for her. I should have picked up the phone when she called, but I was hurt. If only I'd have picked up the phone. If only she hadn't walked home…none of this would have happened." Dad sniffed. "I know she'll say yes now, though. And…and maybe over time she will love me. I owe her this. I have to find that ring. The quicker we marry, the less time anyone will know. Mary doesn't want anyone to know about the baby. Not even her parents."

Pain twisted in her chest, sucking the breath from her. Blood drained from her face, and she slowly pivoted. "What baby?" she whispered.

"Where is that ring? I have to find it."

Brigitte's feet remained glued to the floor as Dad's cryptic words pierced their way into her brain. Mom had walked home from somewhere because Dad hadn't picked up the phone. Something bad had happened—the reason he continued to apologize for not being there. Something Mom never told. Instead, she'd married Dad—a man she only wanted to be friends with. But his offer helped her conceal a secret.

A secret baby.

Mom had hurt herself when Brigitte was ten. But not because of something that happened when Brigitte was ten. But before Brigitte was born.

Brigitte. Brigitte was her secret.

Her knees buckled, and she collapsed on the half-tossed mattress. But the brooch. If the killer took it at the attack, then how was it in the picture when Brigitte was ten? "Dad, have you found Mary's brooch?" It was a risk asking. The timeline didn't make sense, though.

"The one she inherited on her birthday?"

"Yes." She played along, hoping for more pieces of truth.

Tears filled his eyes. "I thought she'd like one just like it. It had meant so much to her. But…but she threw it off the side of the mountain. Oh, Mary! I'm so sorry. I should have been there. I didn't mean to upset you again." He slumped in a chair. "I thought it would make her happy. Remind her of her grandmother. I just want to make her happy."

Brigitte sat beside him, put her arm around him. "I know." The original brooch was a gift passed down. The killer took it. Dad must have made a replica and given it to Mom as a present on their anniversary trip to Big Bend when Brigitte was ten. But she couldn't handle it

and threw it away. That's why Brigitte had never seen it in person. Only in that one photo.

"What's he talking about?" the nurse asked.

"Something that isn't going to calm him down. He'll need some help, I'm afraid."

And so did she. Brigitte bolted from the room. She didn't want to be alone. Not now, when her world was tipping and nausea exploded from her stomach into her throat. She turned to the one source of solace who hadn't rejected her and had her full faculties.

Mrs. Kipling.

Lightly knocking on her door, she heard the permission to enter and stepped inside.

"It's me. Brigitte."

Mrs. Kipling wore a soft white-and-pink housecoat with matching pink slippers. She sat on her bed, her hand resting on her braille Bible. "Of course it is, honey. I'd know your voice anywhere. I also know it's shaky. Has your father had another episode?"

*She* was having an episode, and it was becoming harder to breathe by the second. "Something bad happened to my mom."

Mrs. Kipling patted the bedside, welcoming Brigitte to come and nestle beside her. She instantly snuggled up. Mrs. Kipling's hand stroked her hair. "Now, tell me all about it."

Brigitte told her everything. She didn't hold back a single thing, including how she felt about Duke. "He kissed me. But he doesn't want a relationship, and I'm not good with them, either. Probably because the man who fathered me is the Sunrise Serial Killer."

Was that why he wanted her dead? Had he somehow figured out who she was? Maybe after he attacked her,

he'd done some cyberdigging on her. Realized where she lived and who her parents were. It explained why the Sunrise Serial Killer didn't employ his usual methods on Brigitte. He didn't want her like he'd wanted the other victims.

He had to know she was his daughter.

If he kept tabs on his living victims, then he would have always known she was alive. But maybe not that she belonged to him. Her parents had married quickly.

"I'm a mess," she said through a strangled cry. Grieving her mother's pain, her father's heartache in loving a woman who'd never actually been in love with him but needed him. Brigitte had never doubted Mom's love... and now, looking back at the sacrifice she'd made to keep her and raise her, she wished Mary was here so she could thank her and tell her how much she loved her. How brave she'd been.

Brigitte closed her eyes as Mrs. Kipling's nails softly massaged her head. "I don't want to be the daughter of a serial killer." The thought of news reporters discovering the possible truth and camping out at her door day and night, the media posting about it and true crime authors knocking on her door to write the story... It all sent a wave of panic into her system.

"Of course you don't. You're not. Not really. You're the daughter of a wonderful man who loves you dearly."

When he could remember her. This was too much to bear. Too much to take in. *God, help me. It's too much for me. I can't... I just can't.*

"And more importantly, dear one, you are a daughter of the Almighty. You belong to Him. He sees you. He knows you. Better than anyone ever will. Lean into Him and trust Him."

That's all she'd ever wanted. To be seen and known. And not to feel so alone all the time, like she had a place to lean. With Dad deteriorating, it felt she'd lost that solid place to rest.

Mrs. Kipling prayed a sweet prayer over her and kissed her head. As soothing as it was, a storm continued to brew inside her gut.

Outside Sunny Days, Duke sat in Brigitte's Jeep, his stomach filled with dread. He glanced at the kit next to him that he'd picked up from the Gran Valle police station after he'd left the hospital. How was he going to tell Brigitte that she was the daughter of a serial killer who was now bent on wiping her off the face of the earth?

He leaned his head back and closed his eyes, praying quietly that God would give him the words and the grace needed to drop this kind of bomb without breaking her. He'd already hurt her with his rejection—even if it was logical and not because of her. It was him. But who wanted the "it's not you, it's me" speech? No one.

Pinching the bridge of his nose and wishing desperately for pain relief that went far beyond his throbbing head, he ran down every scenario in his mind. None of it ended with Brigitte being okay.

His cell rang. Vera. His colleague had a way of calling at times he didn't want to talk. But he answered, as she might have information. "What's up?"

"Just wanted to call and check in," she said. Baloney.

"I have a predicament." He told her what he'd found out at the hospital.

"Ooh. That's tricky. Just go in there and do the job with the kindness you always show to witnesses and victims."

"Yeah."

"Unless…it's far more personal than professional?" She let it hang.

"I care about her. More than I've cared about anyone since Deena. And even then, it's…different. I can't explain it. But we've already had a conversation. She doesn't have the extra time to pour into a relationship, especially one that would be long-distance. Too much traveling back and forth."

"And what about you?"

"Me? I'm not getting married again. Falling in love with her wouldn't be fair. Besides, she's never been in a long-term relationship."

"Sounds like you're in a pickle, then, Duke, since it's obvious you're already falling in love with her." She sighed. "Can I say from experience that when it's real, go for it. Because you never know when it's going to be ripped from you, when it'll all burn up in flames. Then you're left with the regret of all the time you should have spent with your loved one, all the things you never said but wanted to, all the miles you wanted to travel together, and in one moment…gone. You have a second chance. Please don't let it slip away, Duke. Not because of her age or lack of relationship experience or your fear. We don't all get second chances."

Duke's eyes filled with moisture as Vera spoke from very real experience. "She's going to hate me for telling her what I have to."

"No, she won't hate you. I talked to Chelsey, and you and I both know she's like some kind of crazy genius people reader. She says Brigitte is good for you. And you'll be good for her."

"Okay," he murmured. "By the way, I detest working with a bunch of coddling women."

Vera laughed. "You won't be for long. Boss just hired a new analyst. A man. Might be the bromance of a lifetime for you."

"Ha-ha. So there's nothing else you need?"

"Nope. Just felt like I should call. Seems I was on point. Take care, Jericho. Let your walls come tumbling down."

"Bible puns. My favorite," he deadpanned. "I'm hanging up now." And he did, then he grabbed the kit and trudged into the assisted living center, his lungs like iron. His cell rang again. Gran Valle police. "Agent Jericho."

"Hi, Agent. It's Horatio. I did like you asked and found a report that might link to your case. It was tough—it hadn't been uploaded into the digital system. I been goin' through boxes old-school style. A woman in Los Artes reported an assault twenty years ago that matches Faith Roswell's report. But she said he took a bracelet from her. Called it a token."

A bracelet. "Silver, with the initials *CS*?"

"Yeah. The victim's name is Christina Sanders." He gave her last known address.

"Thanks, Horatio."

Duke hung up and made his way down the hall until he reached Mrs. Kipling's room. The door was open and Brigitte had snuggled beside the older woman. He wanted to be able to comfort her in his arms.

He knocked lightly on the open door, and Brigitte sat up. Her eyes were red-rimmed and puffy, her nose pink. "I saw you as I was walking by," he said gently.

"Hello, Agent Jericho. You're welcome to come inside."

"Thank you. Good to see you again." He glanced at Brigitte, and her sight trailed to the DNA kit he held in his hand. Her eyes glistened again, and she inched toward him, holding eye contact, tears sheening her gorgeous gray eyes.

When she reached him, she said nothing. She simply opened her mouth.

She already knew.

He opened the kit, put a pair of latex gloves on, then took out the long Q-tip–looking swab and uncapped it. "I'm sorry," he whispered as he carefully swabbed the inside of her cheek as tears ran down her face. "I'm so sorry."

After capping the swab and replacing it in the kit, he slid off his gloves and, boundaries being tossed out, he pulled her to him and wrapped her tightly in his arms, resting his head on top of hers. They stood that way for what seemed like eternity, Mrs. Kipling murmuring prayers in the distance.

"How did you know?" he finally asked.

"My dad. I put the pieces together." She shared the pieces with him, then they said their goodbyes to Mrs. Kipling and he promised to visit her again before he left for Quantico.

They entered the game room and took the table in the corner they'd sat at when he'd first met her. Seemed like yesterday and forever ago. The smells of coffee and cinnamon filled the stale air inside the big room.

"I don't know what to think. My mind is a jumble of unprocessed thoughts and fear." She rubbed her temples and then stared out the window. "I just found out about him. He must have done the math, knew I was his, but I don't understand why he'd want to kill me... I mean,

I know he's a vicious killer and they're as warped as they come, but still…"

Another layer of disturbing news Duke didn't want to unload on her already overwhelmed psyche. "Brigitte, I don't think he recently discovered you. I think he's known about you all along, if he hand delivered cards to your mailbox. He kept up. He saw you."

"I know, but why not kill me then?" Brigitte's face paled, and her hands tremored. She balled them until they were white-knuckled. "Why now? Because I interrupted him? It doesn't make sense."

Duke swallowed the mountain in his throat. "Before, you were like a piece of jewelry. Valuable. A treasured trophy, and now… I'm afraid you're DNA evidence that could potentially link him to these murders, especially to your mom's assault."

The statute of limitations was up on those who had survived, but there wasn't one on homicide.

"So he recognized me in the desert. Realized he'd have to take me out since I was now involved and may have known about the brooch, and as a cop, I'd piece it together—or you would and do exactly what you just did. Take a DNA sample."

"I think so. It fits his change in MO. And he then realized he was better off killing any early victims or witnesses—which is why he killed Faith. I don't think it was accidental. Neither was shooting at Hannah Harker. Which means Christina Sanders isn't safe."

Her face twisted in confusion for a moment. "CS. The bracelet."

"Horatio found the report. Hadn't been uploaded digitally. He had the brains to check the old boxed-up case files."

Brigitte raked a hand through her hair. "What if someone didn't want it uploaded? Kept it buried on purpose."

Detective Chris Collins.

# THIRTEEN

Brigitte hunkered down on her bed with her mom's favorite afghan up to her chin. Duke had made her a cup of tea earlier and made sure she was good, then he had to get the DNA sample sent off. He wanted to do it himself, not trusting anyone not to tamper with it. His friend at the lab had promised to do a rush on it due to the dangerous circumstances.

Chris Collins. Raphe LaMont. Both suspects, and one of them might be her biological father. It was surreal in a scary, never-going-to-wake-up kind of way. If it was Raphe, she knew where her talent came from, and it made her want to puke.

She'd cried herself to sleep last night. Emotionally and physically drained. The sun had been up for a while now, but Brigitte didn't have the energy to roll out of bed. But Duke would return soon, and she had a job to do.

If only Dad was in his right mind, she could ask him more questions and get direct answers.

She forced herself out of bed and made herself presentable. Her phone beeped. Text from Mina LaMont.

Her check for the painting she'd recently sold was at the gallery.

She texted back she'd pick it up. She needed the five hundred dollars. Bills weren't going to stop coming because her life was upside down. While she had her phone in hand, she sent a group text to Patricia and Terry to congratulate them on baby Wheaton and said she'd be by as soon as she could.

The sound of a car in the drive signaled Duke was back. Brigitte unlocked the door, and he slipped inside. "I thought you might be sleeping still. It's okay to take the day for yourself."

"Nah. I'd rather occupy my mind with work. I need to run by the gallery and pick up my check. I kinda hope Raphe isn't there. That's gonna be weird. Creepy."

"We don't know that it's him." He opened the front door, she exited and he locked it behind them. "After the gallery, I want to go see Christina Sanders. I have her address."

"I never even asked what the doctor said about Mom."

"We'll talk about that later."

Meaning he didn't want her to know. He was protecting her, and she appreciated it immensely. It was nice to have someone to lean on. Unfortunately, there was no future except friendship for them.

"You want to drive? It's your Jeep."

"Nah. I'm too distracted." She chose the passenger side, and they drove to the gallery. Raphe's Benz wasn't out front. Didn't mean he wasn't here. Inside, Mina stood behind the white half-moon desk. She glanced up and smiled.

"You look tired."

"I feel tired." She shrugged, and even that felt heavy.

"I got some new paintings in to replace the ones I sold. You have anything new?" she asked and handed Brigitte a white envelope.

"I haven't had much time to paint. Wish I did. I'll let you know. Where's Raphe?" She scanned some of the new art. Mina must have brought it back with her from Los Angeles.

"Running errands. He'll be back later. Why? You need to talk with him?"

"No," she said and wandered around the small gallery. Abstracts, mostly. One of lips. Another of a pair of female eyes. It was stunning. Intricate.

"Talk about an eye for detail, pardon the pun," Mina said through a smile. "I can't decide which of that artist's pieces I love most—the eyes or the one of the hand."

Duke moseyed over and studied the painting with her. "I like the eyes. They remind me of yours."

Brigitte snorted. "These eyes are green."

"Yeah, but if you look closely, you have that same outline around your iris. Kinda looks like the Christmas star."

"It's called a starburst pattern," Mina said. "The artist who painted it says it's unique. Raphe really found a gem with this artist. He has an eye for talent. Pardon the pun again."

Brigitte felt far from unique. "I got mine from my mom."

Suddenly she and Duke exchanged the same knowing glance.

*A lovely star before sunrise.*

All the victims had gray eyes in common. What if they'd all had the starburst pattern around their eyes, too?

"Are you thinking what I'm thinking?" he whispered.

"That we found another common denominator? But I read the coroner reports, and there was nothing about a starburst pattern. But the fact they're lying in the desert with stars in their eyes watching the sun rise makes more sense than ever before."

Their killer might be obsessed with this pattern—fixated, even. "Mina, is that pattern rare in an eye? Do you know?"

"Oh, I have no clue. I'm not an eye expert."

An optometrist might have some answers. Brigitte was clueless about how eyes were made or why those patterns existed or even if they existed in everyone. "What's the name of the artist who painted this?"

"Benny Zadeira."

"In LA?"

"No, actually. El Paso. You want to buy it?"

"Maybe." *No.* But she didn't want to tip off Raphe, and Mina might tell him Brigitte had been asking questions about eye patterns. If he was the killer—and her biological father—he'd know she was on to him. "Thanks for your help."

They calmly walked to the Jeep before speaking freely or showing any excitement that a case might be breaking. "We need to talk to Christina Sanders. If the killer is now aware and taking out old victims, she's next. We need to make sure she's safe. Her place isn't far from here, and then we need to talk to that artist about those eyes."

"Absolutely," Duke said. "I don't remember seeing anything in the reports about a special eye pattern that went along with their gray eyes."

"Gray eyes are rare. I imagine these particular pat-

terns are, too. We might be better off talking to an eye specialist."

"Agreed."

Brigitte turned the air up in the vehicle as Duke gave her Christina Sanders's address. Five minutes away from the gallery. In no time, Brigitte drove into a small subdivision sprinkled with stucco homes with terra-cotta roofs. They walked up the narrow sidewalk to the front door and rang the bell.

Nothing. She rang it again. Finally, the door opened, and a woman not much older than Brigitte appeared with a towheaded toddler on her hip. "Can I help you?"

Duke revealed his creds, and Brigitte showed her badge. "We're here to see Christina Sanders."

The blonde's eyes narrowed, and she cocked her head. "Christina left a month ago. She moves a lot. I'm her cousin, Adria."

Moves a lot. "How often does she move?"

Adria shook her head. "Maybe every six months to a year. She's in El Paso right now."

If the killer sent anniversary cards, then it was possible Christina moved to avoid them. But this time she'd kept her address, allowed her cousin to live here—maybe even pay rent—and skipped town. The killer might believe she still lived here. "Has she received any mail lately?"

"Funny you should ask that. Yesterday, a card was in the mailbox for her. I texted her, and she said to throw it away. It's in the trash."

"Can we have it?" Duke asked.

Adria frowned. "It's in the can on the street. They come later today."

Duke beelined it to the can. "Which bag? Do you know?"

"Last one I tossed in this morning."

Duke retrieved the bag and opened it, his nose scrunching as the smell of rotting garbage wafted from the can. He immediately saw the card and snatched it. He opened it. Brigitte walked over and looked.

A simple anniversary card. No writing. No signature. Nothing on the envelope but food stains. A blank reminder of what was likely the worst time of Christina's life. "I keep an evidence bag in the back. You never know." Brigitte grabbed it and brought him a plastic evidence bag with a red seal.

He dropped the card inside and sealed it. They returned to Adria at the front door.

"Can we have Christina's El Paso address?" Duke asked.

"What's this all about? Is she in trouble?" Adria asked.

"Not at all. She might have information pertaining to a case we're investigating, is all." Duke kept his hands open and to the sides. Brigitte had grabbed a travel bottle of hand sanitizer from the Jeep console, and she handed it over now.

Adria gave them Christina's address. Not too far from the community center where Kayla had taken classes. "Is Christina an artist? Or has she taken any art classes you might know of?"

"Not that I know of. Like I said, she moves a lot."

"Thank you for your time."

Back in the Jeep, Brigitte's cell phone rang. Sunny Days. She answered the phone. But it wasn't about Dad. It was about Mrs. Kipling. She finished the call and hung up. "Mrs. Kipling tripped and broke her arm and

ankle. She'll need surgery on the arm. They couldn't reach her son. I'm all she's got. Drop me at the hospital then go on to El Paso. Keep me posted. I'll stay with Mrs. Kipling until Vance can get there."

They headed for Gran Valle, Brigitte hoping this fall wouldn't set Mrs. Kipling back and that Duke would get some new information that would help them break this case. But so far, nothing had worked out to their benefit.

"How will you get home?"

"I can ride back to Sunny Days with Mrs. Kipling in the ambulance if necessary and stay there until you get back. I'll be fine."

"I worry."

She worried, too, but she'd be in a hospital surrounded by people. "Don't. It'll be fine."

"I'll call when I know something."

"Visit that artist, too. He might be helpful about the eyes. In the meantime, I have Google." She grinned, and he held her gaze.

"See you soon."

She nodded and then jumped out. Duke moved to the driver's side as she rushed inside the hospital to be with Mrs. Kipling, praying God would help them to find this killer before it was too late.

Duke wiped the sweat from his brow as he stood outside Christina Sanders's apartment. "Who is it?" a shaky female called from the other side of the door.

"FBI special agent Duke Jericho, ma'am." He held up his creds for her to view behind the peephole.

The door unlatched and three separate locks clicked, then a woman in her mid- to late fifties opened the door. Wiry gray hair hung over her shoulders; she wore

glasses with chunky red frames. She was dressed in black yoga pants and a long, baggy T-shirt printed with kittens.

"How can I help you? Is it about the neighbors? I don't know much other than cars come and go all night. But I've never actually seen drugs."

He glanced next door, then back. "No. I'm here about something else. And I apologize if it stirs up some bad memories."

With a pale face and shaky hands, she allowed him inside. The home was tidy and modest and smelled of vanilla. He noticed a candle burning on the coffee table and a half-eaten sandwich.

"Have a seat," she said in a strangled voice.

Duke retrieved a picture of the silver bracelet from his phone and showed it to her. "We've been investigating a case, the Sunrise Serial Killer. Are you familiar?"

She nodded and glanced at the bracelet.

"We saw a report you made over twenty years ago about an attack and a bracelet he stole. Is this the bracelet?"

Again, Christina nodded. "You think…you think the man who hurt me is the same man who's been murdering these women?"

"I do. This bracelet was found on one of the earlier victims, and no one could place it. Until now. Could you tell me about that night?"

"I really don't want to. I went to the police because my boyfriend made me. But there was nothing they could do." She shrugged and told him about that night. "So I just tried to move on and forget it."

"Your cousin Adria says you move a lot. Is that because of the cards he sends each year?"

Her eyes filled with tears. "Yes. I think I finally outran him this time by renting to Adria. She wires me the money, and I use cash everywhere I go. I clean houses—cash mostly." Her eyes suddenly widened. "Is he going to kill me?"

Duke couldn't bring himself to frighten her with the truth. The killer appeared to simply enjoy terrorizing them from year to year. But he couldn't say one way or the other. "I would be cautious but not overly concerned." He noticed she had gray eyes. A little bluer than Brigitte's.

The pattern.

"This is going to seem odd, but can I see your eyes up close?"

Her hands reached her throat and pressed. "He told me I had eyes like a star before a sunrise. Or something like that."

"I don't mean to make you uncomfortable."

"No…it's fine."

Duke opened the blinds behind her and looked closely into her eyes. It was there. That starburst pattern—not identical to the drawing or to Brigitte's, but it had a similar Christmas star outline. It wasn't simply gray eyes, but the pattern.

Who would notice those things? "Have you let someone paint your portrait or take your picture?" A photographer might have a lens to get close enough.

"I've had photos taken but never painted. Why?"

"Did you have your portrait taken any time in the year before your attack?"

She stared at her clasped hands on her lap. Finally she shook her head. "No. Not that I recall."

She wore glasses. "Did you see an eye doctor or get

frames made a year before your attack?" An eye doctor or someone who fit people for frames would have a nice close-up view. Especially using the lights to study pupils and irises.

"I went yearly. But to a specialist. I have a condition. It was sometime before the attack. I stopped seeing him after. I moved to San Antonio."

Duke did the math. Was it even possible for the Sunrise killer to be an eye specialist? He'd been hurting women for well over two decades. He would have had to be young—or someone who worked in the office. "What was his name and where was he located?"

"Oh, I still see him now that I'm back in El Paso. Dr. Stanley Hanover." She gave him the address. "But it wasn't him. Dr. Hanover always smells like a tobacco pipe, and the man who hurt me smelled like a strong aftershave."

"Thank you. We're going to do our best to get him."

"I hope so." She followed him to the door, and as she closed it behind him, he heard the locks click one at a time. This woman hadn't felt safe in twenty-some years. Duke prayed he'd find the killer and return some measure of safety to this woman.

He drove the twenty miles to the eye clinic and waltzed inside. "I'm looking for Dr. Stanley Hanover. FBI special agent Duke Jericho." He showed his creds, and the woman at the front desk jumped up.

"I'll get him."

Even if Dr. Hanover wasn't the killer, he might be able to shed some light on the unique eye pattern. Duke stood in the reception area, two patients trying not to stare at him. Frames lined the walls, and in the center of the area, a man sat working on frames. A man with

salt-and-pepper hair came out in a doctor's coat and handed the man a piece of paper. He glanced up and made eye contact with Duke and nodded a greeting.

The woman from the front desk returned with a balding man behind her, who said, "I'm Dr. Hanover. How can I help you, Agent Jericho?"

"Can we talk in private?"

"Of course. Come on back to my office."

Duke followed the fit but older doctor to the offices. He sat in a chair across from Hanover, who perched in his plush office chair behind his meticulously organized walnut desk.

"Christina Sanders told me she sees you for an eye condition."

"She does. Saw her as a child through her twenties, then I believe she moved, but about three months ago she came back. Is she in trouble?"

"No." Duke wasn't ready to start asking incriminating questions. If he was the killer, he'd clam up. But if he was obsessed with the gray eyes and the starburst pattern, he'd love talking about that. Duke would read his body language and tone. "But I was wondering about her unique eye pattern. It might help me in another case."

"What eye pattern would that be? I see a lot of patients, and I can't remember every detail of each one."

"The starburst pattern."

"Ah. Eyes are unique. In fact, more unique than fingerprints. The starburst pattern is rare—as are gray eyes. A person with both would be a very rare find."

Which would explain why the killer's time frame ranged from a year between kills to several years.

"But even the pattern will be different with each

person," the doctor continued. "Eye patterns are genetic as well."

He had to reveal some of his hand. "Why can't these patterns be seen in corpses?"

"The iris is a muscle, and when a person dies, it relaxes, resulting in a fully dilated pupil with no visible iris at all."

He wanted more information on Dr. Hanover before asking for patient files and all that went with naming him as a person of interest.

"Can I ask why the interest?"

Duke stood. "Working on a case where the eye color might be important. Might not." He shrugged nonchalantly. "Who knows? One runs every angle when desperate and out of road to drive down."

Dr. Hanover grinned. "Understood."

They shook hands, and Duke let himself out, glancing back at the eyewear section.

If all the victims had eye issues and had seen Dr. Hanover, he was definitely going on the suspect list. But it was possible that someone less prominent, like a frame fitter, might be a more likely suspect.

He needed to find out if the other victims wore glasses or had had an eye appointment in El Paso prior to being targeted.

And he needed the information three days ago. Time wasn't on their side.

# FOURTEEN

$B$rigitte had dozed off as Mrs. Kipling slept. After surgery, she'd been sent back to the rehabilitation wing in the assisted living center. It was late. She checked her watch. After nine. Duke had called and checked in earlier. He'd filled her in on his visit to El Paso and said he was coming back to Gran Valle to go through the files and make phone calls about victims visiting eye clinics or needing new frames.

In the meantime, he'd run a check on Benny Zadeira, who had painted the green eyes with the starburst pattern. He was a local of Los Artes. Fifty-nine years old. Taught a few art classes and had a degree in art history. Tomorrow, they'd interview him. Duke had his team digging into any connections to the victims. Five dead. Three who had survived—one her mother.

Brigitte had apologized for not being much help to him, but Mrs. Kipling needed her. Vance had called and checked in, sorry for not being able to get there, but he'd been held up at work. She understood. She guessed. Who was she to judge?

Mrs. Kipling stirred and opened her eyes. Brigitte leaned in. "You thirsty?"

"Yes."

Brigitte helped her drink from a straw. She looked frail and exhausted.

"Thank you for being with me. I know Vance would be here if he could." She smiled and pushed the cup away. "What time is it?"

"Almost nine thirty. Duke is about to pick me up, but if you need me to stay the night, I'm happy to."

"Oh, honey. You don't need to do that. I'll be fine. The Good Lord is watching over me. He's watching over you, too."

"I know." She sighed. "Doc says you'll mend. Clean break in your ankle. Your arm needs a little extra TLC. You scared me."

"I'm sorry for that. I do appreciate you coming. You know, besides Vance, you're the only one I have left." She shifted. "I've looked. Back when my sister needed a kidney transplant, we looked for family through one of those sites. I wasn't a match. She died before she could get one. She was my last living relative aside from my son."

"I'm sorry to hear that. You've got me as long as you want me." She held Mrs. Kipling's hand.

"Where's that agent who smells so good and sounds like a dream?"

Brigitte chuckled. "Working the case."

"Any leads?"

"Maybe." She released Mrs. Kipling's hand as a shadow cast darkness in the hall. She expected Duke to enter, but nothing. A tickle at the back of her neck had her standing up, watching. "He thinks the killer might be a photographer, an artist or even an eye doctor."

"My second husband was an ophthalmologist. You

can imagine how upset he was to know I was going blind, and he was unable to heal me. Vance tried to follow in his father's footsteps, but it didn't work out."

"Oh? Did he not enjoy that line of work?" She continued to stare at the shadow. Was someone standing in the hall casting a shadow, or was a light out?

"Not ophthalmology. Art. Edward, Vance's father, was an artist and often in his head. His talent was unbelievable. He created the most beautiful picture of the Chisos Mountains. It's still over my bed, isn't it? In my room?"

Brigitte assumed it had been hung there by the living center. "Yes. It's lovely."

"I told you he began drinking and could be quite awful, especially when he was being hard on himself as an artist—if a painting didn't sell. To me and to Vance. Broke Vance's heart and even more his spirit. He wanted to follow in his father's artistic footsteps. Then Charlie came along. He was a good father, though it wasn't easy to parent Vance. He still longed for Edward. When he was thirteen, I let Charlie adopt him. Things got better, and Vance went into the same line of work as Charlie."

Brigitte glanced at Mrs. Kipling. "Vance is an optometrist?"

"Ophthalmologist. That's why he couldn't get here. Surgeries, though he does less since his accident. Many patients. I'm so proud of him. If it wasn't for him catching my condition early, I'd have been blind sooner."

Brigitte's insides twisted. Vance worked in El Paso but had been born and raised in Los Artes. His father had been a gifted artist.

Brigitte had that same gift.

"How…how old is Vance exactly?"

"Fifty-four this year."

Knees buckling, she grabbed ahold of the bedrail. The shadow moved, and Vance Kipling stepped into the room—no cane, walker or scooter. Broad shoulders. Dark eyes, focused on her, and his finger on his lips to hush her as he motioned with his chin to his mother. In his other hand he held a gun.

Surely he wouldn't hurt his own mother. His eyes held a malicious warning.

"Is someone there?" Mrs. Kipling asked.

"No, ma'am. Just us," Brigitte said shakily as her insides bounced around. "I believe Duke is waiting for me." He should be here. He'd said it'd be about nine forty-five. "If you need anything, just call me."

"I will, dear. I hope you catch this guy. Be safe."

Vance's lips pulled back, showing a row of perfectly straight teeth; it was the insinuation behind them that was crooked and sharp.

"I'm sure we'll find him."

She slowly moved toward him to spare Mrs. Kipling. When she reached him, his fingers dug into her arm, and for the first time, she noticed they shared the same chin and coloring.

"Hello, daughter," he breathed quietly in her ear.

"Don't call me that. You are not my dad."

He jerked her into the empty hall, the gun concealed by a blanket the nurses would assume he was bringing to or taking from his mother. It poked into her ribs, and her head turned fuzzy. She needed to remain calm and levelheaded. She'd look for a way to escape when it was less dangerous for the residents…for her own father, who was in great danger and didn't even know it.

"Where are you taking me?" she asked as he smiled

and pushed ahead, maneuvering to the south-side back entrance. "And how're your feet?"

He chuckled. "I got that from Ted Bundy. Clever, huh?"

"You're saying you were never in a car accident? You're faking?"

"Did you ever suspect me? And no one would like this. No one in El Paso matters, and it's not like my mother would know if it was true or not."

"No." But she wouldn't have suspected him anyway. She hadn't known his profession or that he had once dreamed of being an artist. "Why did you take my mom's brooch off Kayla? And how long have you had it?" She needed answers and time to hatch a plan to get away.

He frowned. "I've had it since before you were born. It was hard to part with. Your mom holds a special place in my heart. She was the first, you know."

Disgust roiled her gut. "Don't you talk about her as if you had some kind of relationship!"

"We had you. I left it with Kayla and then regretted it. Decided to keep it, but dropped it when I heard you. Then I was afraid if I left it you'd connect it, and I hadn't wiped my prints from it yet. I'm always extra cautious. Had no choice. I was less than happy about that." He pressed the gun farther into her side, and she winced as they walked down a long corridor. Nurses coming in and out of rooms. No way to make a move yet. Not without getting people killed, and she'd been responsible for enough injuries and deaths.

But her dad hadn't been incoherent. He had given Mom another brooch to replace the one Vance took. But it had been too much of a reminder of that night and her

reaction had backfired. She'd thrown it over a cliff instead of being happy to have one like it. Then not long after that trip, she'd tried to end her life.

"You know," he said, "I've known about you, kept up with you all these years. My own flesh and blood. Better than jewelry. But I knew once that FBI agent hit the pavement and you figured out who the brooch belonged to… I knew I had to destroy you."

"Well, it's too late. I already took a DNA sample. It'll match the evidence you left behind on the earlier victims and they'll know. So killing me now is stupid."

He gripped her arm until she cried out from the acute pain. "Shut your mouth. Is that any way to talk to your father?"

The word *father* sent a wave of nausea and rebellion through her. "Or are you just jealous the artistic talent skipped a generation?"

He pushed her out the door and smacked her face, the burning sensation reaching her head. "I said shut up."

But he'd released her arm. She punched him in the face and sprinted toward the east side of the building. If she could make it to the front and the parking lot, Duke would spot her.

She just had to make it to Duke.

Something hard smacked the back of her head, and she dropped to the ground and into blackness.

Duke checked the time. Past nine forty-five. An unsettled feeling in his chest sparked a wave of panic. He texted Brigitte to see if she needed more time.

No response.

His phone rang. What in the world was the lab doing calling this time of night? He answered.

"Hey, Duke. It's Sheila. I said I'd come through and do a major rush. I did. You owe me a steak dinner. That swab you sent in—it's a familial match to the DNA left behind on the victims. I uploaded to an ancestry site and got a hit to a Victoria Kipling. Both the swabbed DNA and the DNA left behind at the crime scenes match with her. I did a search, and Victoria Kipling's only surviving relative is a son. Vance Kipling."

Gut churning, he put the pieces together. Did Brigitte have any idea that the reason she felt connected to Mrs. Kipling was because she was her actual grandmother? How in the world?

And she was in there with her right now.

Not answering.

"Thanks, Sheila. One steak dinner coming up. I gotta go." He ended the call and raced into the building, stopping at the nurses' station. "I need Mrs. Kipling's rehabilitation room. Now." He showed his credentials, and the nurse spouted her room number. "Have you seen Officer Linsey?"

"Not since she came in. I did see Mrs. Kipling's son, though. He came in about ten minutes or so ago."

Duke's head spun, and his heart jackhammered against his ribs. "Thanks. If you see him again and with Brigitte, put this place on lockdown. He may be armed and dangerous." He sprinted toward the rehabilitation wing and barged into Mrs. Kipling's room, gun in hand.

No sign of Brigitte. Or Vance.

"Who's there?" Mrs. Kipling asked.

"It's me. Duke Jericho. Can you tell me how long ago Brigitte left?" He tried to remain calm, but it wasn't working. Brigitte was far too personal to him, and she'd

been taken from right under his nose. He'd never forgive himself if something happened to her.

"I don't know. She did seem a little off when she left. It couldn't have been too long. What's wrong? Is she in danger?" Mrs. Kipling's voice shook, and she sat up straighter.

No point lying. Right now, he needed Mrs. Kipling's help, and if that meant breaking the news that her son was a monster, then so be it. Brigitte's life was more important than Mrs. Kipling's hurt feelings.

"Mrs. Kipling, I think the Sunrise Serial Killer might have her, and I need your help."

"Me?" She clutched her chest. "Oh, dear. How can I help?" Her lower lip quivered.

"Mrs. Kipling, I'm sorry to inform you, but your son, Vance, is the man we're looking for. Can you tell me where he works or where I might find him?"

Her lip quivered and she clutched her chest. "He's an ophthalmologist. In El Paso."

Duke blew out a breath. He didn't have much time. "Do you have a picture of him?"

"Well, no. Not here. I—I can't see."

Duke wanted to kick himself. He wasn't thinking straight. "Where is his office in El Paso?"

"The Daylight Eye Clinic."

Time froze. The doctor who had nodded to him in the eye clinic—the one with salt-and-pepper hair talking to the framer. He grabbed his phone and looked up the eye clinic directory. Dr. Vance Kipling.

One and the same.

He had the right place, the right idea, but the wrong doctor.

The Sunrise Serial Killer took his victims and kept

them for an extended period, but Brigitte wasn't a target—she was evidence, and his daughter, so his ritual and style would be irrelevant. Duke had no idea where he would take her or if she was even alive at this moment.

"I can't believe that Vance would hurt anyone. He's a good boy, Agent, and he fancies Brigitte. He says she reminds him of the daughter he never had. I think that's sweet. Are you sure?"

Truer than she even knew, but revealing all he knew would cost him more time than he had. "I am. Do you have any idea where he would go?" Going back to his home would be too risky.

Tears leaked from her eyes as her mouth gaped. "I'm so sorry. I have no idea." She wiped her eyes. "Why would he want to kill her?"

Duke sighed. "She's evidence against him. I promise to be more forthcoming when I can, but time is of the essence. Help me think of a place where he goes that might be sentimental to him. Secluded."

He dumped bodies in the desert around the Los Artes and Gran Valle area, but that was a lot of ground to cover, and Duke couldn't be sure that he'd take Brigitte to the desert.

"Well… I know he liked to go with his father when he was a child to paint. Edward only took him a few times, when he hoped Vance had the same artistic talent. He didn't." Her voice quivered.

"Okay. That's good." It was a starting point. "Where is it?"

"Once you go past Los Artes city limits, there's a long stretch of highway that has an access road that turns off into the desert and mountains. It's quiet and

secluded. Edward liked to be out there for hours. Uninterrupted." She sniffed. "I'm praying for Brigitte—that you'll find her—and I'm praying for my son."

"Thank you, Mrs. Kipling. And... I'm sorry."

Duke blew through the front doors and raced to Brigitte's Jeep, praying if this was where Vance had taken Brigitte, that Duke would make it in time.

Head pounding, Brigitte opened her eyes to darkness. Her hands were bound in front of her as she lay on her side in the middle of the desert. Stars twinkled against the inky canvas of night. Vance stood to the side of her.

"Do you know where you are?" he asked quietly.

"The desert."

He spun on her, his eyes narrowed. "Don't be a smart mouth, Brigitte," he said with a father's disapproving tone. "My dad used to bring me out here. I wanted so much to be like my father."

"Yeah, well, I don't."

He let out an exasperated breath. She was pushing the envelope, but if she was going to die, she wasn't going to let him know she was terrified. That much he wouldn't get from her.

"He painted the most beautiful paintings. I idolized him. One day we came out here and I had a canvas, too. I was so proud of my creation, but he looked at it and his disappointment hit me in the gut. But it was his words that stung deep. Told me I'd never be a painter. Didn't have an ounce of talent and it was shame. Not long after that, he left us. He left because I couldn't paint."

"You don't really believe that, do you?"

"Why not? It's true. Parents leave their children.

Your mom tried to leave you when she slit her wrists in the tub."

Fury burned inside her. "No, she was trying to leave you and what you did to her! You're a monster!"

He laughed through his nose. "Maybe. And maybe I can't create artistically the way my father did. But I do create art. I couldn't create stars in a night sky before dawn...but I saw the starlight in your mom's eyes when she came for an eye exam. I was fresh out of optometry school, working toward ophthalmology. Gray eyes like twilight. And the starlight in them. I couldn't resist possessing that beauty. And then I saw it again in Denise Govern and Christina Sanders...and the others. Right before they died, their eyes dilated and that was art. I made that happen."

"You murder women. You're not an artist. Artists respect beauty, not possess it. You're sick."

"I respected them. Laid them out to watch the sun rise."

"Dead people can't see, you idiot!"

He knelt in front of her and thrust a finger into her nose, pushing until tears formed. "I didn't want to kill you. I created you. But you haven't given me much choice." He tucked her hair behind her ear, and she flinched. "You...you have what I've always wanted. And it's unfair. It's wrong."

What did she have that he wanted?

Artistic talent.

"My father would have loved you. And that's why I hate you." His hands came around her throat and squeezed.

She kneed him in the groin, and he released her neck. Rising up, she headbutted him and awkwardly clam-

bered to her feet, then bolted. He might be in good shape, but she was a trained officer. Adrenaline helped keep her moving. She didn't look back, just hauled it toward a road. There had to be one somewhere. She hurdled a cluster of cacti, footfalls heavy behind her.

The road was up ahead.

Car lights shone.

She kept running until she was in the middle of the road and the vehicle slammed on its brakes.

The door swung open, and Duke hollered her name.

"He's right behind me! It's Vance Kipling."

"Get in the car. Call in backup." He ran past her and into the desert. She dug in her console, found a utility knife and cut her hands free, then called in backup, giving them the location best she could. Then she grabbed the gun she kept in the glove box and ran back into the desert to help Duke.

A gunshot split the arid night.

Brigitte lost her breath. Up ahead, a figure loomed over a heap on the desert floor.

"Duke!"

# FIFTEEN

*Three months later*

Brigitte unloaded the sacks of groceries on her kitchen table. She had to start doing better about eating right, and for the past two months, Mrs. Kipling—her grandmother—had been coming over for dinner on Thursday nights.

The night she could never forget, she'd hovered over her biological father's body on the desert ground and felt nothing but relief. Relief that he was dead and could no longer torment or kill, and relief that Duke was alive. Vance had raised his gun first, but Duke had fired first.

Vance could have killed Brigitte. Fast and quick. He hadn't shot her as she made a run for it, and she'd never know why—nor did she care. She'd never be able to understand how anyone raised by a God-fearing, precious woman like Mrs. Kipling could turn out to be a heinous monster.

The news media had gone into a frenzy once it hit the public that the Sunrise Serial Killer had been Brigitte's father and it was Brigitte's work on the case, in tandem with Special Agent Duke Jericho, that had brought jus-

tice to so many women, including Brigitte's mother. She was being bombarded with TV opportunities and even book deals to tell her story.

Brigitte wanted nothing to do with it.

Instead, she'd painted her feelings and given them to Raphe and Mina to sell in the gallery. They sold like hotcakes, especially when Raphe and Mina had used her story for marketing efforts. Oh, well. Nothing she could do about that. As far as she knew, Raphe was still stepping out on Mina—or not. Not her business.

Detective Chris Collins had retired early after Jamie's family caught wind he hadn't filed a formal report or pursued the lead on her stalker and they threatened to sue.

Dad had been having a few lucid days, but mostly he asked for Mary and continued to apologize. Now that Brigitte knew what he was sorry for, she'd told him that Mom forgave him for not answering his phone and making her walk home. That seemed to settle him for a time. The sad truth was Vance Kipling stalked his victims, and if that opportune time hadn't been there, he would have found another.

Brigitte and Victoria—that's what she was calling Mrs. Kipling now—had been bonding even more. She wasn't ready for *Grandma*, though she'd felt like a granddaughter all along. God had seen her. God had cared about how lonely she felt, and in His great wisdom and providence, He'd given her family she'd never known about.

The day after Vance's death, Duke had finished up his part of the case, then hugged Brigitte and told her goodbye and to call him if she ever needed anything—including her pilot light lit.

Did needing *him* count? Every day for the past three months, he was all she thought about. The way he made her laugh, think. Now that her eyes had been opened to her mother's past and the trauma, she understood Mary's distance and the depression. Brigitte had brought her childhood pain into her adulthood and jumped out of relationships for fear she'd be hurt or hurt someone else.

And it was too late with Duke. She hadn't fought. He'd have to realize that he couldn't keep carrying his pain, too, or he'd never trust or love again. And that wasn't something she could fix by telling him. It was a revelation he needed personally. And a desire to move forward.

After unloading the groceries, she gathered up her supplies and drove out to her spot to paint. She wasn't going to let tragedy and fear rob her of her favorite place and her love for the arts or the desert. It was who she was. She couldn't help that.

Today, she'd paint how she felt about Duke. In blues and grays and pops of yellow. He'd once told her that she painted hope without knowing. But in this case, it would be false hope.

Instead of pining or whining, she'd paint, get to know her grandmother even better and continue taking care of Dad. Cap had reinstated her, but she chose to stay on leave for a while longer, and he understood. She needed time to deal with her past, seek some counseling and breathe. She had a teeny nest egg left, and her paintings were selling and bringing in some decent money.

Who knows, maybe she'd never go back into law enforcement and see if she could make painting a full-time gig.

The sound of footsteps reached her ears, her heart lurched into her throat and she spun around and gasped.

Duke Jericho stood in jeans, cowboy boots that did him oh, so much justice and a T-shirt that hugged his broad chest and defined biceps. "I should have known you'd be out here," he said with hands up in surrender. "Nothing scares you, does it?"

She stood, unable to speak, in total shock and heart palpitating from surprise and elation.

Duke didn't wait for a reply; he stepped toward her. "You know what scares me?"

She shook her head, still unable to speak or to breathe. It had been three months since she'd laid eyes on Duke. What was he doing here now?

"The way I feel about you." He ate up half the distance between them. "Every day I wake up thinking about you. Every night I fall asleep thinking of you. Doesn't help that your *Desert Moonlight* painting is hanging over the TV in my bedroom. First and last thing I see every morning and night."

Duke had bought her painting? The one she didn't think would sell but did—to him. Her mouth fell open.

He moved a few feet closer, enough so she caught his fresh-showered and subtle cologne scent. "But I can't do it, Brig."

"Can't do what?" She finally forced herself to speak.

"Say goodbye to you. And mean it." He closed the distance between them. "I came here to work a case and call it a day. But I fell in love. Didn't want to. Didn't mean to. Told myself I was too old for you—and maybe I am. Maybe you will have to take care of me when I'm geriatric. I'm selfish enough to let you." He smirked.

"Told myself it wasn't worth the pain to love again, but I think it hurts worse trying to not love you."

Tears burned the backs of her eyes. "You bought my painting."

He chuckled in that way that made her heart beat faster and her stomach dip. "And I told you I loved you."

She grinned then sobered. "What about your job? And the distance?"

"Funny you mention a job… I'm in between them right now. So not only am I offering you an old man—I turned forty a couple months ago—I'm offering you a jobless one, too." His right eyebrow inched north. "Hard to say no to that, huh?"

"You quit your job?"

"I did. But I'm sure something will turn up. I have friends in El Paso and now here in Gran Valle and Los Artes." He shrugged. "A detective position is open at Gran Valle."

He'd quit his job and was coming here.

For her.

Everything in her leaped and danced. "I love you. Old and broke."

"Well, I never said I was broke. I said I was jobless." His smile undid her, and she threw herself into his arms.

He framed her face. "I want a future with you, Brig. I want to get to know your grandmother. I want to help you with your father, help you bear that burden. I want to fix your broken appliances and maybe even learn to paint. Bob Ross makes it look pretty easy."

"You want to make happy little trees?" She snorted through a laugh.

"I want to make *you* happy."

He just did. "I am. I am so happy."

His lips met hers, painting a masterpiece that revealed a promising and glorious future. When he finally broke the kiss, he wove his fingers through hers and looked up. "See those two big clouds up there?"

"I do."

"What do you see?"

She tried to make out some kind of animal or picture, but nothing came. "I don't know. What do you see?"

He laid his head on top of hers. "I see you and me. Forever."

"For a man who never played the cloud guessing game, you're pretty good at it."

"I have a good teacher."

His arms came around her, and she'd never felt more seen or known. Not just by Duke, but by God, who saw not only what she needed…but whom. He'd taken heartache and tragedy and painted a perfect picture of hope.

Brigitte didn't need the grays and dark blues to paint. Her future was far more colorful and vibrant than that.

\* \* \* \* \*

*If you enjoyed this Quantico Profilers story by Jessica R. Patch, be sure to read the previous book in this miniseries,* Texas Cold Case Threat.

*Available now from Love Inspired Suspense!*

Dear Reader,

Sometimes we can all feel unseen and forgotten, especially when we are faced with difficult situations, challenges and adversity. Know that God always sees you. He is always for you. And nothing can separate you from His love.

I love to share fun book news and more spiritual encouragement with readers, so please sign up for my monthly newsletter to get Patched In at www.jessicarpatch.com and connect with me on BookBub!

Warmly,
*Jessica*

# LOVE INSPIRED

*Stories to uplift and inspire*

---

Fall in love with Love Inspired—
inspirational and uplifting stories of faith
and hope. Find strength and comfort in
the bonds of friendship and community.
Revel in the warmth of possibility and the
promise of new beginnings.

Sign up for the Love Inspired newsletter
at **LoveInspired.com** to be the first
to find out about upcoming titles,
special promotions and exclusive content.

---

### CONNECT WITH US AT:

 Facebook.com/LoveInspiredBooks

Twitter.com/LoveInspiredBks

## DEFENDING FROM DANGER
*Rocky Mountain K-9 Unit* • by Jodie Bailey

Multiple attacks aren't enough to scare off wolf sanctuary owner Paige Bristow—especially once she calls in her ex, K-9 officer Reece Campbell, and his partner, Maverick, for protection. But will a secret connection between Reece and Paige's daughter threaten their attempt to stop the danger from escalating into something lethal?

## TEXAS BURIED SECRETS
*Cowboy Lawmen* • by Virginia Vaughan

Publicly vowing to bring a serial killer to justice, Deputy Cecile Richardson solidifies herself as the criminal's next target. Can Sheriff Josh Avery keep her safe long enough to identify and catch the culprit—or will the killer successfully hunt down his prey?

## CAVERN COVER-UP
by Katy Lee

Suspecting her father's murder is linked to a smuggling ring sends private investigator Danika Lewis pursuing a lead all the way to Carlsbad Caverns National Park. Teaming up with ranger Tru Butler to search the caves for the missing artifacts is the fastest way to uncover the truth that a killer will do anything to keep hidden.

## SABOTAGED MISSION
by Tina Radcliffe

When an investigation leaves CIA operative Mackenzie "Mac" Sharp injured and her partner presumed dead, Mac must hide to survive. But her fellow operative and ex-boyfriend, Gabe Denton, tracks her down—leading a well-connected enemy straight to her. Now with someone trying to frame and kill her, Gabe's the only person she can trust.

## SHIELDING THE TINY TARGET
by Deena Alexander

Accepting help from Jack Moretta is widow Ava Colburn's last chance after her late husband's killers track her down and target her little girl. Ava's been running from these murderers for years, and Jack could be just what this family needs to put the deadly past behind them once and for all...

## HIDDEN RANCH PERIL
by Michelle Aleckson

After witnessing her aunt's abduction, veterinarian Talia Knowles will do anything to find her—even as the kidnappers set their sights on her. Could relying on neighboring ranch hand Noah Landers be the key to finding her aunt and discovering the culprits' true motives?

---

LISCNM0622

business card. He lifted it and read the message. *I see the sunrise in your eyes every time I look at you.* \* *R*

He held up the card that had literally slipped through the cracks. Probably been missed by the police's original search. He almost didn't see it. "Well, this is interesting."

# FOUR

Brigitte sat across from Duke at the Los Artes precinct combing through Kayla Lowe's phone records with a yellow highlighter in hand. She'd found one number within the month prior to Kayla's murder that wasn't there previously. The incoming number had called once a week, at random times, and each call only lasted a few seconds. Could be a prank call by the Sunrise killer. She'd highlighted the number. "I'm gonna have the number traced. See who it belongs to. No outgoing calls to the number."

Duke absently nodded as he searched victim photos and noted pieces of jewelry on their bodies, as well as any mentions of jewelry missing in the reports by family or friends. Simply from observation, it was clear that Duke was meticulous, and when he was fully involved in an activity, it had all his attention.

Wonder what that looked like when he was focused on a woman?

"Then I'm going to call David Hyatt." He might have some useful information, since Kayla had attended his art class in El Paso.

Another absentminded nod.

"Then I'm going to put myself out there as bait. Lure the killer into plain view." She waited a beat, then hid her grin when he whipped his attention onto her face, his intense dark eyes holding hers.

"Not a chance."

She allowed the smile to make its way onto her face. "Ah, so you hear when it's critical."

His hard lines softened, and his shoulders relaxed. "Ha-ha. Sorry. I can get lost in my work." A hint of sorrow sent the corners of his lips into a droop and flashed through his eyes. As if it had cost him something important. She wondered if it might have cost him his marriage. He had said he was divorced. Was he there but not present, like her mother had been with Dad?

"I understand. I can get that way when painting." Which scared her, because what if she was the one who couldn't be truly present in a romantic relationship and not the other way around? "Each stroke of color is a step toward the goal, and once I see it taking concrete shape, nothing else matters for a while. Just me and the canvas. The need to see the whole picture." Brigitte wouldn't risk hurting someone like Mom hurt Dad, like she'd hurt Brigitte at times.

Duke grinned. "Exactly. You'd make a good detective. It's similar. Only instead of a painting, it's a puzzle. One you're piecing together. The goal is justice. The portrait is the perpetrator of the crime. I suppose it's one of dark shades and not so much bright color."

Brigitte's heart sped up, and heat filled her cheeks. Duke got it. Understood. It was just like that. Yes. She'd never thought about detective work, not really, but she did love solving puzzles. "Canvas is a little like a puzzle. Each color I paint is a piece. Each piece connects to the next until it's a picture."

He nodded. "I suppose that's true." Duke held her eyes, and another wave of heat flushed her insides. How did she feel this connected to a man she barely knew when she had a hard time connecting with her own family or other men she'd dated? She broke eye contact for fear he'd read her thoughts and her attraction to him—not only physically, but an emotional attraction that overwhelmed her even more. She stood abruptly, and the chair teetered. She righted it, cleared her throat and felt the burn of embarrassment scrape her throat. "I'm gonna go check that number."

As she strode to the door on wobbly legs, she felt his gaze resting on her, but she refused to turn around. She hurried to Dispatch and had them trace the number.

No number popped. No address.

She poured a foam cup of water and brought one to Duke with the news. "Burner phone," she said as she set his water on the table.

He thanked her and frowned. "It appears he was harassing her—even if it was only heavy breathing or a single threat. If he enjoys psychological threat, we might find a unique number with some of the other victims as well. I don't see phone records pulled in some of the earlier cases, but I do in the last two vics' files. Nothing highlighted. Maybe they weren't looking for what we are."

"I can go over them while you finish with that, and I need to see my dad before dinner. I know he won't remember, but I like to try and keep consistency in any way I can, and visiting at the same times helps. At least it helps me."

Duke handed the phone records over, and his finger brushed hers. "I'm sorry, Brigitte. About having to go through this with your father. Alone. Going through any pain is tormenting, but to do it alone…if you need anything, even to talk, you can talk to me. I'd understand."

Was this guy for real? It meant so much to hear those words. Mrs. Kipling offered her prayers and support, but since Dad's illness and Mom's death, she'd retreated into herself. It wasn't like church family hadn't reached out through calls, food or texts, but she hadn't met their efforts. She wasn't sure why other than she'd always felt alone even when she wasn't, and why should now be any different?

"I appreciate that, Duke. And for your understanding. I know we have a serious case to handle. Every minute is a minute he gets away and targets a new victim."

"Family has to come first. I said that already. I learned the hard way, and I'm not making that mistake again or letting someone on my team make it, either." He smirked. "I guess we are a team."

So maybe he had neglected or been distant from his wife. "For now." She nodded and slipped into her chair, grabbing the yellow highlighter and reaching for the case files. She needed the dates of the murders so she could track a month prior.

"For now," he murmured and sipped his water.

They worked silently, only the sounds of the highlighter raking across paper and the shuffling of case files and photos and the squeaking of the dry-erase marker on the board as Duke jotted notes and drew lines to connect dots. After an hour of working together in the quiet comfort of each other's presence, Brigitte grabbed the blue dry-erase marker.

"Here's what we have."

Duke raised his head and nodded for her to continue.

"Victim number three, Jamie Harker, received one call a week on the same day for four weeks before she was murdered. Same number. Probably a burner phone. However, the two victims before her didn't receive any phone calls from the same number that I couldn't identify as friends and family, and not in that once-a-week, same-day-of-the-week pattern. Victim four, Adley Portman, also received calls starting four weeks before her murder, just like Jamie Harker and Kayla Lowe. All three different numbers—different burner phones."

Duke rolled a pen between his fingers and looked upward. "Maybe he decided to add phone calls and used untraceable phones to up his torment before he murdered them. Even killers evolve, need more to fuel their sick agendas. Either way, good work. Kayla told the florist shop owner she'd been stalked. Victim four, Adley Portman, noted to her sister that she felt like someone was watching her and had even been in her car. Stalking may also be part of his MO and the other vics never reported it or confided in anyone."

"We should ask in case those questions weren't asked back then, not until Adley Portman's sister noted it."

"I agree. Maybe someone remembered a lurker or a new friend but didn't connect it."

"I could sketch a profile if they do and even progress it a decade or so to help us with a face." Anything she could do to help catch him, she'd attempt. "What about jewelry? Any notes about missing jewelry or accessories added that didn't belong to the other victims besides Jamie Harker?"

"Yeah, actually. The second victim, Debbie Deardon, was found with a silver bracelet and the letters *CS* inscribed on the inside. Police asked about them, but Debbie's mom—who she lived with—didn't know anyone with those initials. They chalked it up to Debbie having a friend her mom didn't know about. But Detective Collins says her friends didn't know of anyone with those initials, and no one at her place of employment did, either. He didn't chase after the lead any further."

"None of our victims have those initials. So they didn't come from one of them."

Duke shook his head. "But he could have stolen the bracelet from someone else and placed it on her."

"He clearly has a freaky jewelry fetish. But how would we even track where he might have stolen the jewelry? Could be off anyone or anywhere at any time."

"It's not a solid lead, that's for sure. I wish we could connect these victims to something more concrete. They appear random."

Brigitte paced in front of the slender conference table. It did appear random, but this killer was diabolical and clever enough not to get caught for decades. Nothing about what he was doing was random.

An hour ago, Duke had dropped Brigitte off at the Gran Valle Police Station, where she'd picked up her own car. She was bummed their interviews hadn't garnered much information other than the second victim, Debbie Deardon, had taken a free two-hour art history class at the Los Artes art gallery about six months before she died. It gave them a tiny dot to connect to Kayla Lowe.

Debbie wasn't a die-hard artist but enjoyed drawing or doodling—as her mother had put it. Mrs. Deardon had no new information about the silver bracelet Debbie had worn at the time of her death, but she had kept it and given it to Brigitte and Duke. It was a simple bracelet with carved designs and the initials etched underneath. Maybe the two letters weren't initials but signified a meaning to Debbie. She could have purchased it herself. Though typically jewelry with engravings came as gifts.

Now, Brigitte parked at the edge of the assisted living home near the walking park for patients. Sometimes she and Mrs. Kipling sat out under the trees and drank lemonade and talked about life, the past and the future. Mrs. Kipling had wonderful stories of faith that breathed hope into Brigitte, especially on days when things felt utterly hopeless and too much to bear. Since Mom had been sick and Dad had been diagnosed with the early-onset Alzheimer's, Brigitte had felt more isolated than ever. God had to have given Brigitte Mrs. Kipling. Every good and perfect gift came from Him, and Mrs. Kipling had been so very good and there at the perfect place and time.

She hurried up the walk; the sun had set already, and she'd missed Dad before dinner. He would be finishing up his favorite TV show and getting ready to go to bed. The lot was sparse. Visiting hours ended at nine, and Brigitte was pushing it.

She entered the side door of the long L-shaped building, the smells of meat loaf and bleach lingering in the atmosphere. The building was quiet as its residents settled in for the night, and she strode past the welcome center, waving at a few familiar faces as she headed toward Dad's room.

As she approached she smacked into Vance—Mrs.